Quail's Tale

Maddy Whitman Mystery Series Book 3

by Carla Howatt and Monique MacDonald

Published by By the Book Publishing.

By the Book Publishing 404, 11716-100 Ave, Edmonton, AB T5K
2G3 Canada First Edition 2025
ISBN: 978-1-7381486-7-7
Cover design by Kaylee Chiument

ACKNOWLEDGMENTS

We would like to acknowledge all the support and help we received from our families. From putting up with us sneaking away for the day to plot the next novel to being holed up in another room, bent over our laptops. They also had patience when we spent most of the day at another book signing or market. Without these two patient and understanding men, this series would not be possible.

Of course, we couldn't do it without our beta readers. These reliable people take the time to read one of our drafts and provide us with input. So major acknowledgement to May Chouéri, Jessie Kerba, Laura Pryatel, Larry MacDonald and Jennifer Mulder.

MONIQUE'S DEDICATION

To all transgender women in my life, your courage is an inspiration. By being your authentic selves, you encourage all women to follow your example.

CARLA'S DEDICATION

To my dad, the best man I know. You've set my standard for men by showing unconditional love for Mum for more than 63 years. I've watched you love, laugh and cry through life, and I am eternally grateful to have been a witness for part of that journey. #TheLongGoodbye

Chapter 1

B e like the bird who, pausing in her flight a while, on boughs too slight, feels them give way beneath her, and yet sings, knowing she has wings. - Victor Hugo

SATURDAY

The storage unit's locker door was stuck again. No matter how hard she tried, Maddy Whitman could not get it to budge, not even a little. She swore under her breath and kicked it as hard as she could. The door popped up a few inches, taunting her.

"Of course, this is what it takes to get you to open," she scowled at the door as she lifted it up. "Well, I won't let you ruin my mood. Things are looking up these days, not even a stupid door could wreck it for me!"

She had recently put a Victorian doll up for bidding on an online auction site. It had been slow to get much attention. After 48 hours, a bidding war had started. It ended with the doll selling for $2,100. This piece alone would pay for her condo and one utility bill for one month. Maddy had come to get it out of storage and package it for shipping. She was bent over a large wooden packing box, trying to pull the top off with the claw of a hammer, when a gruff male voice coming from behind startled her. She jumped up in surprise.

"Where's my stuff?"

"Pardon me? Who are you, and what stuff are you referring to?"

"You know damn well what stuff!" The voice belonged to a red-haired man who looked like he could have been a lumberjack, right down to his plaid green and black shirt, thick beard, and toque on his head. "Don't play me for a fool, girly."

"Okay, settle down. First of all, I'm nobody's 'girly'. Second, you need to tell me exactly what you are looking for. I buy lots of things, all the time. Thirdly, you'd better change your tone of voice if you want me to help you." She did not know who this guy was, and she certainly was not going to allow anyone, let alone a fresh-out-of-the-bush lumberjack, to disrespect her.

"I'll speak to you any way I want to. You took MY stuff from MY locker last Wednesday. I want it all back, NOW!"

"Last Wednesday? I didn't pick anything up... Oh yeah, wait." She remembered having won a storage auction that had been held right here at the Triple A storage facility. It had been a small one. The locker was full of junk that needed to be taken to the dump. No wonder she had forgotten about it. The only thing that had been worthwhile was a binder filled with hockey cards. She sold those easily to a collector who owned a store in West Edmonton Mall. She could always count on him to buy sports cards and memorabilia from her.

"Are you referring to the hockey cards?" she asked him.

"Damn right, I am. And all the engine parts too."

"You'll have to take that up with Rod, the manager of this place. He's the one who puts the lockers up for auction."

This was not the first time Maddy had to deal with an owner who had been delinquent in his locker rental payments. After three months, storage facilities often put the contents of unpaid units up for auction. Maddy made a living buying and selling the contents she won in live and online auctions. She usually sent upset former owners to the various storage facilities' management, or, if she still had the items, she would sell them back to them for a fair price.

"I did. They told me you were here and that I should bring this up with you." Maddy noticed that his tone had not improved. "I want it all back, now," he said, taking several steps closer to her.

Maddy was going to kill Rod, Triple-A's facilities manager.

"Stay right where you are. I didn't invite you into my locker." His aggressive demeanor was starting to worry her. "Look, mister, I don't have your things anymore. Sorry. If I did, I'd sell them back to you. Now, could you please leave?"

If looks could kill, Maddy would have been dead on the spot. The lumberjack guy balled his hands into fists and started coming toward her. She took several steps back into her locker, trying to put distance between them.

"You had NO right selling my things. No right at all! I had five hundred dollars stashed in that old exhaust pipe!" He quickly advanced on her.

"Actually, I did." Maddy tried to distract him while looking for something she could use to defend herself. "Look around, do you see any of your things here?" She spotted a frying pan she was meaning to take to Goodwill lying on the floor a foot away from her. In a pinch, it would do. "Why hide your money in old rusty parts anyway? Who does that? You should be grateful that it wasn't five thousand dollars. There's a lesson in there for you."

"Don't try to waste my time. You have to give me all the money you got for my stuff AND that five hundred dollars."

He leaned forward and grabbed her arm, pulling her toward him. She curled her fingers toward the base of her palm and, using the momentum she had from the pull, she smacked him in the face as hard as she could. He immediately let go. "You shupid bits! You boke my toot." Blood was dripping from his mouth. "You gomma bay foh dish." He lunged at her.

Maddy screamed for help, then grabbed the frying pan. Lifting it high, she used all the strength she could muster and hit him hard on the head. His knees buckled, his eyes went wide with a look of shock and then rolled to the back of his head as he collapsed onto the ground.

Zane, her friend, occasional business partner, and Canada goose co-parent, came running in.

"Maddy, are you okay?"

"I think so," she replied, still holding the pan. "Did I kill him?"

Zane bent down to take a closer look at the crumbled body. "Nope, he's still breathing. What the hell happened? I heard you scream and came as fast as I could."

"This dipshidiot wanted his stuff back. Rod told him to come and see me. By the way, when I'm done here, Rod's going to meet the same fate. When I told this guy that I'd sold his things, he grabbed me. So, I let him have it."

"You certainly did, by the looks of it." Zane grinned. "You know, you're sure full of surprises. Never a boring moment with you around."

"I could do with a dose of boring right about now," Maddy sighed.

"Here, let me help you tie him up before he wakes up. Then we can figure out what to do with Mister Tough Guy."

"Thanks. Here are some zip-ties. Please, don't let me leave without taking this pan with me. It's found a new forever home, right by my front door, next to my trusty baseball bat."

"THEN I SMACKED HIM, hard. I tried to do what they showed us in that self-defense course we took together last month. Remind me to thank Rick, by the way." Rick was Maddy's brother by choice. She was describing the morning's events to her best friends, Ashley and Tasha, over coffee. Ashley was smart, no-nonsense, beautiful, and oozed class. Tasha was a fun, energetic, and passionate Italian woman with street smarts, and she happened to be Rick's wife.

"Did it work, Bella?" Tasha asked.

"Yes, and no."

"What do you mean?" Ashley looked down at her as she stood pouring them each more coffee.

"I aimed for his nose with the palm of my hand, like this." She showed them how she had curled her fingers just so. "Guess he was closer than I thought. I hit his mouth instead."

"Well, that explains the bandage." Ashley pointed at Maddy's right hand.

"Yeah, his teeth cut and bruised my hand. It hurt like heck."

"Bet it hurt him more than it hurt you." Tasha smiled and lifted her hand to give her a high-five.

Maddy went to high-five her back, then decided to switch hands and use her uninjured left one instead. They all laughed. "Then Zane called the cops. They came and hauled Mister Lumberjack away. I'm definitely pressing charges!"

"Zane was there?" Tasha lifted an eyebrow.

"He heard me yelling for help. He was too little, too late." She shrugged her shoulders. "Anyway, you won't believe what else happened!"

"There's more news?" Tasha asked, even though she was not one bit surprised. Maddy always seemed to attract drama.

"Please, do tell Mads," Ashley said.

"Guess who's dating?" Grinning, Maddy wiggled excitedly in her chair.

"You?" Ventured Tasha.

"Nope. Guess again," she said, not taking the bait. Her grin grew wider.

"Just tell us, already! You know I'm not good at guessing games." Ashley picked up the latest copy of House and Country magazine sitting on the coffee table and flopped down on the couch.

"Fine," Maddy sighed. "Shirley and Bob."

"Who?" Tasha asked.

"Aunt Shirley? From Triple A storage?" Maddy looked from one to the other, expecting them to figure it out.

"Doesn't ring a bell. What about you, Ash?"

"Nope, I got nothing," Ashley replied as she flipped to the collectibles section of the magazine.

"Oh, c'mon, you guys! Ash, you do know Bob, from Bernard's? The antique and collectibles store on 124th Street?"

"Oh, that Bob! I do know him, he's an older gentleman," Ashley nodded. "Sweet guy, quirky son, Nick. No Nicky... No, Niko!"

"Yeah, anyway, Aunt Shirley is Rod's aunt and the owner of Triple A," Maddy explained.

"I've heard you mention Rod quite a few times. Isn't he the guy who looks like Danny DeVito's cousin?" Tasha asked.

"That's the guy!" Maddy said. "Aunt Shirley suddenly dropped everything and headed for Hawaii to elope. She left Rod to run things. She even left wee Engelbert with him."

"Wee Engelbert?" Tasha looked confused and horrified. "She abandoned her little boy? What kind of woman does that?"

"Oh, come on! Do you guys not listen to a word I say?" Maddy threw up her hands.

"Not when you start going on and on and on..." Ashley teased, winking at Tasha.

"Small fellow, with a couple of scraggly hairs on his head?" Maddy continued, ignoring Ashley. "Engelbert, Bertie? Missing a few teeth. Nasty disposition?"

"Hold on a minute. Bertie? Never heard of him before. He can't be Aunt Shirley's little boy, though, not if she's Rod's old auntie." Ashley was paying attention now. "Who is he, in relation to Shirley and Rod?"

"He's Aunt Shirley's," Maddy said. "I can't believe you don't remember me talking about him. He's adorable but has a nasty habit of taking a poop when you least expect it."

"What?" Tasha and Ashley said in unison.

Maddy's eyes widened at their response, and she looked again from one to the other.

"Why do you know his bathroom habits?" Tasha asked.

"Umm... I've seen him do it all the time. The voiding process is natural, guys!"

Ashley stared at her friend before finally asking, "Who or what exactly is Engelbert, Maddy?"

"I told you that already. He's Aunt Shirley's! She got him from the Humane Society. She tried to tell Rod he was an Alberta Special. He thought that meant he was a fancy designer breed." She giggled. "He didn't understand that it meant Bertie was a mongrel." Maddy laughed some more at the memory of her breaking the news to Rod.

"The fact that he's a dog would have been a good thing to lead with Mads!" Ashley tossed the magazine in her direction.

"Well, what else would he be?" Maddy replied, lifting her arms and ducking to avoid being hit by the flying collectibles issue. "You don't think I would describe a kid like that, do you?"

"Let's say we were a bit confused," Tasha said.

"And, yes, you actually would," teased Ashley.

The three women looked at each other and burst out laughing. The absurdity of the exchange and the visual of a person randomly going to the bathroom on the floor appealed to their occasionally childish sense of humor. After they wiped their tears and got themselves under control, Maddy continued her story.

"According to Aunt Shirley, when she went to Hawaii, her new husband was distracted by all the hot hoochie mamas sauntering the beach wearing next to nothing. Before long, he left her for a 57-year-old hussy. Her words, not mine. And ran off with her money."

"That's awful!" Ashley said. "Having your heart broken is one thing, it's a whole other amount of hurt to be robbed at the same time".

"She didn't seem so worried about the money, though. She kept talking about how he also took her Betty Boop collection. I got the impression she was more broken-hearted about that than him leaving her."

"So, how did she end up with Bob?" Tasha began nibbling on a bowl of chips sitting on the end table. Her eyes were fixed on Maddy, hanging on to her every word.

"Bob was staying in Hawaii with a friend who had won the lottery. His buddy took him along to see if they wanted to move there. He happened to be in the same area as Shirley. One night, feeling a bit lonely and at loose ends, they both attended what they referred to as a 'pineapple singles night'."

"A WHAT?" Both Ashley and Tasha exclaimed.

"Hey, I'm just repeating what they told me." Maddy held up her hands, palms facing her friends. "Don't shoot the messenger. Especially an injured one."

"Did they know that a pineapple is sometimes the symbol for swinging?" Ashley asked.

"I asked them if they knew what it meant, and they looked at me like I was crazy. They said that obviously, it's a symbol of Hawaiian hospitality, which is why they are often used as décor on door knockers, welcome mats, etc. I didn't offer them the alternate meaning."

"Oh, my gawd! Bob's son and Rod must have been mortified when they found out." Ashley said, putting a hand on her face.

"Wow," Tasha murmured.

They sat there, grinning at each other, as they imagined the elderly couple showing up at a swingers' party without even realizing it.

Chapter 2

MONDAY

"**G**oing once... going twice... sold to the man with the spikey hair!" the auctioneer declared with the authority of a major general at the Triple-A abandoned lockers auction.

"Congrats, Zane!" Maddy walked over to fist bump him with her left hand.

"And congratulations to you, too. I noticed you were successful in purchasing lot #49." Zane smiled, pointing his auction brochure at her.

"Yup, and Rod was kind enough to tell me that once I've paid for it, he'll take it to my locker for me."

"Wow! It must be nice to get such white glove service. Wish I was a pretty girl," Zane chuckled. Maddy felt herself redden slightly.

"I wouldn't go as far as calling it 'white glove' service, I'm pretty sure he'd do it for anyone who asked," Maddy insisted. "He's a very nice guy, once you get past all the bravado."

"Doubt he'd do it today. Several lots are being auctioned off here." Zane pointed at the brochure again. "I agree, though,

he is a good guy and all, I just can't see how he would have the time to help everyone who needed it."

"Hey, by the way, did you notice that Aunt Shirley's back?" Maddy changed the subject to something a bit less focused on her.

"I heard that. I'm a bit surprised, I thought she was supposed to be in Hawaii indefinitely. She got married, didn't she?"

11

"Yeah, she did; however, it was short-lived. He left her for a hussy," Maddy said poker-faced.

"Oh, really?" Zane chuckled, then pointed over Maddy's shoulder. She turned around and noticed Rod approaching them. The wind blew his combover, making it appear to be gently waving at people as he passed by them. Engelbert was nestled in his arms, his chin on Rod's forearm, gummy overbite sucking on Rod's sleeve cuff.

"Hi Rod," Maddy said.

"Hey Maddy, I've got all your auction treasures moved into your unit. I convinced the auctioneer that I knew ya and that you were good for it. You can go pay him whenever you're ready," Rod said, looking up at Maddy.

"That's awesome, thank you so much!" She avoided Zane's 'I told you' look while Rod talked to her about her latest lot purchase.

"Anytime," Rod said, beaming. "You know I don't mind helping you. If you need anything, anything at all..."

"I hear your aunt has returned from Hawaii, Rod," Zane interrupted, grinning at Maddy. "You must be happy to see her."

"Well, yeah, kinda," Rod said hesitantly. "I was a bit shocked. We stayed up late last night talking about everything, and we've come to an understanding."

"An understanding?" Maddy's curiosity was piqued. "Yeah, things will continue as usual. Aunt Shirley wants to remain retired, but she'll be living on-site with me." Rod said. "Like roommates, not like me shacking up with my aunt or anything."

"Of course, no explanation needed," Maddy replied, trying to avoid visualizing Rod 'shacking up' with Shirley. "It can be nice to have another adult around sometimes."

"Exactly," Rod said, relief plainly showing on his face, glad Maddy didn't think any less of him for living with his aunt.

"Well, I'm going to leave you two gentlemen to chat while I go see what's in that new lot of mine."

MADDY UNLOCKED HER storage unit door. She noticed that it wasn't sticky anymore and rolled up without effort. That pleased her more than anyone could imagine. Rod must have fixed it. She had to make sure to thank him.

'Zane might have a point,' she thought. 'Then again, who am I to complain if it makes him happy to help me? Why dissuade him?' Switching the light on as soon as she entered, she looked over her shoulder, making sure no lumberjack was lurking in the shadows. She did not want a repeat of the other day. Her storage locker also doubled as her makeshift office. The space was packed. There was no room to move around much. Bins were piled on top of boxes, and random items were strewn everywhere. It was an ongoing battle for her to keep her stock rotating as much as possible. More than once, she'd discovered something underneath boxes, items she was unaware she even owned.

"Oh, what I would not give to have my very own proper store," she mumbled, bumping her hip on the corner of a dresser as she made her way through the unit. "Damn it!" She rubbed the tender spot and carefully reached for the bin Rod had placed on the top of the pile. As she pulled it down, the stacked boxes beneath it began to sway. She quickly put the box she was holding on the ground, freeing her hands to stabilize the rest. She silently promised herself to review her finances and see if she could afford a small store somewhere, even a tiny one would do.

She pulled the first clear bin out in the open and began rummaging through it. Something caught her eye on the auction page when she had surfed it. It looked like no one else had noticed it. She pulled out the piece of china that all had missed, but she had seen. It was very hot on several collectors' markets right now. No one else had paid any attention to that particular locker's lot. She had waited it out and purchased the whole lot for $55. If that one piece was what she thought it was, she would double her money quite easily.

"Eureka!" she exclaimed after turning the serving tray over and inspecting the bottom. It was exactly as she had thought, a Royal Crown Derby piece. Not the best find she had ever made, nevertheless, it was a good start. She felt that anything else in the box would be gravy. Excitement mounted. She always got a little flutter in her stomach when she sorted through a new bin's contents. She began to pull out an array of items, including salt and pepper shakers, a couple of smaller pieces of china, and a box that held what appeared to be someone's silver collection. That could be a nice find if she could track down just the right buyer, someone who made rings and such out of silverware. That was assuming they were silver. People didn't buy silverware to use as flatware anymore. However, they seemed to like it when it was transformed into jewelry and wind chimes. Digging further into the bottom of the box, she spotted a leather scroll-like package, tied with a leather string.

"What have we got here..." She loved surprises, that moment of opening up the unexpected, that second just before the object revealed itself. She had tried to explain it to PopPop, her step-grandfather, whom she considered her real grandfather and only living relative. He just didn't get it. She even tried to compare it to his love of coin collecting. He told her that he needed more excitement in his life than coin collecting these days. She promised herself to bring him along to auctions more often. She didn't want him looking for 'excitement' in the wrong places. She'd heard about lonely seniors who suddenly started behaving like teenagers. Maddy certainly didn't need that to worry about.

She turned her attention back to the leather roll. Inside was a set of sharp-looking knives. They gleamed in the fall's warm afternoon sun. 'What a nice find,' she thought. They looked like quality knives. Maddy was pretty sure they could bring a nice amount of cash. This was something that needed to be investigated further. She rolled the knives back up and set them aside, then replaced the other objects in the plastic bin. She would come back later to take pictures of these objects to accompany the ones to be listed for sale.

ONCE BACK HOME, SHE sat at her dining room table with her laptop by a large window and began listing some of the items she knew the value of, like the platter. Once that was done, she started researching the knives. First, she took a picture of the knives, then she did an image search. So many results came up that looked very close to the set she had, yet were not identical. The prices ranged between $20 to $2,000 each. Not helpful enough. On the bottom of the leather knife roll was a faint signature. Unfortunately, she couldn't make out what it said. Frustrated, she quit her research and put them away. She would take them later to Bernard's and see if Bob might know anything about them.

She reached for the overly ornate lamp that was sitting on her kitchen table and took a picture of it. She proceeded with researching it like she had with the knives. An incoming call interrupted her. Her cell displayed the name of an annoying person she occasionally did business with. She half-sighed, half-groaned. She was expecting this call, even so, she never enjoyed talking with the caller on the other end. The woman was usually quite an unpleasant person to deal with. Still, she was one of Maddy's best customers. She was an interior decorator and buyer who often purchased high-end items for her clients.

"Hey there, Paris," she answered, then put her on speaker phone.

"You called earlier. I was in a very important meeting with one of my top clients. Priorities, you know." Paris' voice oozed with attitude, each word coming out in a clipped, curt tone. "You left a message for me to return your call. Make it quick, I have another meeting soon," Paris said.

"Yes, I did. How are you doing today?" Maddy smiled as she spoke, trying to trick her body into believing this woman didn't get on her last nerve.

"I'm fine. Did you have something for me?"

"I'm not sure, I'm sending you a picture via text. It's an ornate lamp I found..."

"Got it." A few seconds of silence passed before she continued. "No, I don't want it. None of my clients would want such a gaudy lamp."

The tone of Paris's voice made Maddy grit her teeth. The condescending snobbishness of this woman was unbelievable. Never wasting an opportunity to let Maddy know that she dealt with a higher level of clientele who had much more discerning tastes than she could ever understand. Yet at the same time, she became very irate if Maddy had a piece with any possible potential at all and did not give Paris the first right of refusal.

"Okay, just thought I'd..." Maddy stopped mid-sentence and stared at the display on her phone. It read 'Call ended'.

Chapter 3

WEDNESDAY

"So, tell me, Rick, what kind of beer do you want this time?" Maddy asked after greeting him with a hug in front of her building.

"Hmm... There are a few new ones out. Surprise me with something from Monolith."

"Oooh, going for the high end, more expensive stuff this time, eh?" she said as she climbed into his truck.

"If it's too much, you can get me whatever. I don't mind."

"I know you wouldn't mind. I'm only teasing you. With all the help you give me, you deserve high-end and more!"

Rick's family had taken Maddy in while she was still in high school, right after her mother died. Life with her stepfather had become a nightmare of violence bordering on sexual harassment. She had always looked at Rick as the brother she never had, the one she had always wanted. He had always been there for her. Rick, his wife Tasha, their twin daughters, and Ashley were her chosen family. "Alright, enough with the compliments. You're gonna make me blush." Rick opened his truck's door for her.

"I don't think I gave you compliments, but if it makes you happy, enjoy!" she teased as she climbed into the passenger seat.

"Yeah, yeah, whatever. What's the plan for today?" he asked while starting the truck. It made a terrible noise. "When are you going to fix that?"

"It is fixed, and I am keeping it that way."

"Tasha and the girls will never ride with you as long as it sounds like that. You know that, right?"

Rick smiled. That was the point. His truck was his alone space, except when he helped Maddy move stuff.

"Directions, m'lady?"

"Triple-A. I need to get rid of a bunch of unsellable, un-donatable junk."

"I take it we are then going to take that load to the dump next, correct?"

"Correct."

"Aren't you going to answer your phone? It's been buzzing for a while now."

"I know, it's just Rod. We'll be seeing him soon. He can tell me whatever it is he wants in person."

"Does he usually call you?"

"Not usually."

"It's buzzing again, might be important."

"Fine, I'll answer. You can start driving, please. You're such a curious cat, you know that?"

"Meow!"

"Hi Rod. What? NO! How? I can't believe it. I'm on my way. Can you call the cops, please?"

"What's wrong?" Rick turned the engine off and looked at her. "Why call the cops?

"Just go! Hurry up, please. Someone broke into my storage unit. Rod said it looks like someone had locked a wild animal in there."

ROD WAS WAITING FOR them at Triple-A's gate. He looked completely demoralized. Maddy jumped out of the truck, and Rick went to park it by the office.

"The police are already at your locker, Maddy," Rod told her. "They were patrolling the neighborhood."

"I just can't catch a break!"

"I'm sorry, Maddy. We'll cover your insurance deductible."

"I'm not worried about that, Rod," Maddy said as they approached her locker. "It's that some of the stuff can't be replaced."

She slowed down as they approached the row of lockers where hers was located. Rick had caught up to them.

"Maddy, it's only stuff," he said. "You didn't get hurt like last time."

"There's been too many times, Rick," she replied, sounding defeated.

She was met by the two officers who were taking pictures and notes. Maddy knew them from some previous unfortunate events and liked them both. Especially Officer Giani Sidhu. She had been kind and patient with Maddy. She had not spent much time with Officer Tom Janvier, but he seemed the decent sort. Seeing them both put her at ease right away.

"Officers Sidhu and Janvier! Thank you for coming so fast."

"Ms. Whitman, it looks worse than it is. We think that whoever did this was in a rush," Officer Sidhu said.

"They made a huge mess here. However, we don't think they found what they were looking for," commented Officer Janvier.

"How can you tell? Did they leave a note?" Rick said sarcastically.

"Yes, as a matter of fact, they did," Officer Sidhu replied, giving him a 'smarten up' look that put him in his place.

Rick looked away sheepishly.

"How is that, ma'am, I mean Officer?" Rod asked, trying to look tall and serious.

"Ms. Whitman, please follow me if you will." Officer Janvier led her to the back of the storage locker and pointed in the direction of a tall Baroque mirror. 'Where's my stuff?' was scribbled on it.

"Ah crap! I bet it's that lumberjack who came in and threatened me on Saturday. The guy you sent my way, Rod."

"Someone's threatened you?" Officer Janvier seemed a bit surprised to hear this.

"Yes, I called you guys, and he was taken into custody," Maddy replied. "I bet he's out on bail already and trying to scare me."

"We'll look into it," Officer Sidhu said. "If it is him, he's going to find himself in some deeper trouble."

"I'll call it in and have someone find him. We'll see if he has an alibi," said Officer Janvier. "Please walk around and make a list of anything missing and of what's been damaged. We will write our report and email it to you for your insurance claim."

"I'd get that door fixed and have a new lock put on as soon as possible," Officer Sidhu said to Rod.

"Absolutely! That's going to be my priority, Officer," he replied, nodding his head up and down repeatedly. He left with the officers, promising to send them a copy of last night's security camera footage.

Maddy and Rick walked around, assessing the damage to her things. It was worse than what the officers had said. Many items were damaged, and some could not be repaired. They grabbed some empty cardboard boxes and started sorting through everything. They separated them into three piles: repairable things, stuff for the dump, and items in good condition.

"You have enough insurance coverage, right?" Rick asked.

"Yes, I do, but they're only likely to pay me the replacement value."

"That's kind of a blessing in disguise, though," Rick observed. "Now you don't have to try and sell them. Plus, you'll get money for the stuff we were going to take to the dump anyway."

"Yeah, it's good in that regard. Unfortunately, some things are worth more than the replacement value," she explained. "I hadn't had time to insure some of the newer items at the collector's value. I just got them this week and haven't had the time to do so."

It took them a good two hours to go through everything and tidy things as best as they could. Thankfully, Rod had returned to help them. He told them the footage had been grainy, but they could still tell the height and size of the person who broke into her unit. They also got a look at the car's license plate but couldn't read it clearly. They hoped that it would be enough to bring Mr. Lumberjack in again for questioning.

"Oh well," Maddy sighed. "Hopefully, this will be the end of him."

"Until you go to court," Rod added.

"You're not helping things, Rod," Rick said, handing him a box to put in the truck.

Chapter 4

SATURDAY

Maddy couldn't believe that it was already Saturday. What a busy week it had been. Two auctions, cleaning the disaster in her locker, taking stuff to the dump, and meeting clients. No wonder time had gone by so fast. This morning, she had decided that it was time to do her much-neglected laundry. While hanging up the last of her blouses in the closet, she heard Dean Martin crooning 'When the moon hits your eye like a big pizza pie, that's amore'. 'That's Amore' was the ringtone she had chosen for Tasha years ago while under the influence of a good Chianti. She shut the door and reached for her cellphone. "Bella! Come stai?" Tasha's voice on the other end always made Maddy smile. "How are you?"

"How would you say 'good' in Italian? Oh yeah. Bene, so far anyway." Maddy laughed at her own reply. "What can I do for you, dearest Tasha?"

"Ashley and I were wondering what you're doing this afternoon. Rick's getting ready to go to Vegas for that car show thing, and I'm needing to indulge in a bit of girlfriend time."

"I'm planning on visiting Ryan at the sanctuary," Maddy said.

"How is our little ducky doing?" asked Tasha.

"Goose! Ryan is a goose." Maddy rolled her eyes. She knew Tasha was bugging her. No matter how often Maddy had corrected her, she always referred to poor Ryan as a duck. Maddy knew she did it to try and get a rise out of her. "He's doing quite well. He's adapted to his lame foot and is learning to run and fly. They're hoping to send him out into the wild blue yonder soon. I'm not entirely convinced he's ready. Zane says I'm being overprotective."

"He does, does he? Is Zane going with you to visit Ryan?"

"Yes, he is," Maddy said. "He has a vested interest in him, remember? Zane helped me rescue Ryan when his flock left him behind because of his disfigured leg."

"Of course I remember, and I'm sure he does care very much about your baby goosie."

There was silence on both sides of the phone for a second or two, then Tasha spoke again.

"How much do you know about this guy, Mads?"

"Know about him? I know he's a nice guy who buys auction stuff at some of the same storage places I do."

"And?""And what?"

"Is that all you know about him? You met him at an auction, and he helped you rescue a lame goose?" Tasha asked. "Well, no..." Maddy answered. "I know that he plays hockey and doesn't spike his hair up when playing because of the helmet he has to wear."

"Okay, and what else?"

"And that's it, okay? Why do I need to know details of his personal life?" Maddy was getting flustered. "Just spit it out, Tasha. What are you trying to get at?"

"Nothing, really. It's just that you seem to be spending an awful lot of time with this spiky hairdo guy, bella." Tasha said. "Have you two started dating without telling us? If that is the case, then you better bring this Zane guy of yours around so we can see if he is good enough for you."

"Don't be silly. We're not dating. Even if we were, he wouldn't require any tests from my best friends."

"Oh yes, he would! Rick met him a couple of times and says he is an okay guy. Ashley, though, has only met him once, and I haven't at all. We haven't properly checked him out yet. He must pass our test."

"He does not!" Maddy couldn't believe she was being interrogated about her friendship with Zane, of all people. She felt that it was time to end this silliness. "All this is beside the point, Tasha. We're not dating."

"Well, if you were, he'd need our approval."

"Good thing you don't have to worry about it then, isn't it? Like I said repeatedly, we are not dating."

"Mmhmm." Tasha was far from convinced.

ZANE ARRIVED PROMPTLY at noon in his old, beaten-up Ford pickup truck. He had one of those carryout trays with two cups of coffee and a large box of Timbits resting on top of it on the seat next to him. The first time Maddy saw him pull up in his truck, she did a double-take. He did not fit the stereotype of guys who drove pickups. That's Alberta for you, she had thought, 'Land of the Pickups.' She climbed in and put the coffee tray on her lap.

"I know how much you like your donuts. Figured we might as well munch on these with our coffees instead of stopping for lunch."

"Good idea! That's so sweet of you. I hate making our little guy wait for us." Maddy was surprised that he even remembered how she liked her coffee.

"I don't think Ryan has a grasp of weekdays, like we do."

"Exactly! He might think we abandoned him or something. Like his real family."

"Don't worry too much about it. We see him every week," Zane tried to reassure her. "I'm certain that he knows we care about him."

"I hope so. Abandonment can affect you for your whole life."

"I feel like you're not talking about Ryan now." He looked at her, wondering who could have abandoned her.

"What I meant is that I can relate, and it's not a nice feeling. Ryan deserves to be loved and cared for."

"The people at the sanctuary are taking very good care of him. You've seen it with your own eyes."

"They are, you're right." Maddy took a sip of her Double Double coffee. "I don't know why I'm being such a worrywart."

"It's because you have a big heart and care about others.

That's something I've noticed about you." He gave her a gentle smile.

"Thanks, Zane." She smiled back. "For the compliment, and for understanding." Maddy was grateful that they had become friends. 'Tasha was so wrong about us being anything else,' Maddy thought to herself. 'How could she even think that about us? Sheesh!'

ONCE AT THE SANCTUARY, Maddy and Zane spoke with one of the keepers. With their help, Ryan had adapted to his foot malformation and had learned to fly. They were confident that he would be able to join a local flock and fly south for the winter.

"Are you sure he'll be able to keep up with the other geese?" Maddy was uncertain about his readiness to venture out on his own.

The keeper smiled, and Zane chuckled. "What?"

"You sound like an overprotective Mother Goose, wringing her hands over her baby gosling on his first day of school," Zane said.

"Ha. Ha," Maddy smacked him lightly on the upper arm. "Seriously, how do you know he's ready?"

"Because he's been taking practice flights around the pond with other geese, he's been eating well on his own, and also..." the keeper looked around conspiratorially. "He told us." The keeper winked at Zane, and both laughed.

"Oh, aren't you two just the funniest," Maddy said.

"We've been doing this for a long time, trust me, he's ready," the keeper replied. "Come on, let's go see him."

Walking through the sanctuary's guest entrance, Maddy noted an array of brochures and posters. She reminded herself that when Ryan was released into the wild, she would need to make a substantial donation to the sanctuary. They did so much good work and greatly helped Ryan when he needed it.

"I swear he's grown six inches!" Zane exclaimed as they approached the enclosure.

"Not likely," Maddy chuckled. Then she caught sight of Ryan herself. "Okay, maybe four inches."

Ryan wasn't a gosling anymore. He had grown into a gander. Time had zoomed by, they had not noticed that their little Ryan was all grown up.

BACK AT HER APARTMENT building, Maddy felt a bit of sadness as she made her way down the hall that led to her suite. The likelihood of Ryan flying south for the winter and her never seeing him again was more difficult to accept than she had expected. This morose mood called for some feel-good TV time. She grabbed her cozy, fuzzy throw and curled up on the couch. She was looking forward to watching old episodes of 'Gilmore Girls'. It usually cheered her up somewhat. At the very least, it would distract her, if nothing else. Pointing the remote at her big screen TV, she was surprised when Netflix refused her login password. She signed out of the account and tried to log in again. It wouldn't recognize the account or password.

"This can't be happening again!" she groaned.

Maddy liked to think she had matured some since the last time this had happened. She decided to take the straightforward route and call her ex-boyfriend, Chad, directly. The last time the password didn't work on his Netflix account she had come up with some convoluted way to solve the problem. It was behavior she wasn't proud of, and she was determined to start acting like an adult. She pulled up Chad's name on her cellphone and pressed call.

"Hi Chad, it's Maddy."

"Oh," he sounded cool and aloof. Not that she blamed him. "Hello."

"I'm here by myself on my couch, and I decided to watch some Netflix," she hoped he wouldn't make her spell it out.

"Yeah, and?" He sounded uninterested. "Did you need a movie recommendation or something?"

Okay, so much for that.

"Umm... no, that's not it. I couldn't sign in, so I logged out and realized it's your account I was watching." She talked in what she hoped was a casual laissez-faire manner, making it sound as though her phoning him and humbling herself was no big deal.

"Uh-huh," he wasn't giving her so much as an inch.

"I was wondering if perhaps you wouldn't mind giving me your new password?" It was best to simply rip the bandage off and come out and say it, she thought. There was a long, painful silence on the other end until Chad finally responded.

"I would if I could, Maddy, but I no longer have Netflix. I guess you're going to have to 'splurge' and get your own."

"Oh, I see."

"Yeah, I got that big promotion I had been hoping for and bought a house in Sherwood Park. I don't have time for things like Netflix any longer. Home ownership is full of responsibilities, you know."

"I'm sure it is." She pictured a long and boring evening ahead of her.

"Listen, since I have you on the phone, would you happen to know anyone who would be able to help me with my house?" he said. "I'm looking to take my decorating up a notch. I intend to entertain more important clients, with large portfolios, at my home. I need someone to source the perfect pieces for me. I thought of Ashley, she's surprisingly too pricey even for my generous budget."

"No, sorry." After this Netflix disappointment, she wasn't in much of a generous or helpful mood. "I don't know anyone off the top of my head. Give me a day or two to give it some thought."

"The sooner the better, please. I need to furnish my home. I don't want it to look like I've put it together with pieces from Walmart or from a used furniture store. You know how vintage isn't my style." His voice sounded a tad too condescending. "I want high-end pieces, not storage locker stuff, if you know what I mean, haha."

Maddy felt her blood start to heat up at this not-so-blatant put-down. He knew very well that most of her furniture were vintage pieces. Then suddenly an idea hit her. She could help Madam Karma kill two birds with one stone.

"Actually, Chad, I know just the person who can help you!"

"Excellent. I knew I could count on you."

"Do you have a pen and paper handy to jot down the contact info?"

"Yes, I'm ready. Shoot."

"Her name is Paris..."

Chapter 5

MONDAY

"I'd love to help you, Maddy, but I don't know enough about these knives to tell you much," Bob said while wrapping up the knives. She had hoped that if she brought them to Bernard's Antiques and Collectibles, Bob would either be able to give her a good idea of what they were worth, or maybe, if she was lucky, he would take them off her hands. If he knew there was a market for certain of her items and sometimes had a specific client in mind, they often made deals on unique finds she had come across in auctions.

"Do you have any idea where I could find out?" Maddy asked. "Someone who may know about these types of knives?"

"Have you checked with your friend, Ashley?"

"No, it never occurred to me to ask her," she said. "She usually deals with works of art or collectible furniture and such. Not kitchen utensils."

"Yes, I know. The only thing I can tell you about these knives is that they're expensive. Because Ashley deals with high-end items, she might be able to point you to someone who knows about collector knives. I'm afraid I don't have any contacts in that area."

"Good point, I'll do that," Maddy said. "So, how is Aunt Shirley doing?"

"Oh, she's doing very well, Maddy, very well indeed. I must tell you, she's such a wonderful woman. I can't believe I've been given another chance at love. Who would have thought a man of my age could fall for someone so hard?"

"That's awesome." Maddy was truly pleased for Bob and Aunt Shirley. No matter the age, it was nice to see people in love. It made her hope that somewhere out there, in the great big universe, there might be someone for her. "We were so surprised that you two even met," she continued.

"Who could have imagined that she would even be from Edmonton? It was meant to be!" Bob clasped his hands and held them close to his heart. "Meeting my little love dumpling was written in the stars."

"Or the pineapples."

"Oh yes, the pineapples! Where would we be without those beautiful ripe-for-the-picking pineapples? Shirley and I are thinking that when we get our place, we will decorate it with pineapples on the door so that everyone will know how welcome they are and that our home is a place of love."

"Wow, that would be something!" Maddy smiled, trying hard not to laugh. Someone will have to tell them about the meaning of pineapples before they put one on their door. It wasn't going to be her, though. She had no intention of bursting their happiness bubble. Or maybe they already knew and didn't want to shock them? Oy vey, she thought, I need a life.

"When are you going to find your other half, my dear?" Bob reached across the counter and placed his hands over hers.

"The world is a happier, brighter place when you have that one special person who makes your heart soar, like my Shirley. How about my son Niko? He's a fine young man."

Maddy had heard the expression 'they had stars in their eyes' before, yet she had never seen someone who embodied it until now. Bob's eyes were practically twinkling. She was sure that if she did not cut this off soon, he would begin gushing and singing a tune from a musical. By the look on his face, tears would not be far behind.

"Niko and I are friends, Bob. I'm afraid there are no sparks between us. Don't worry, I'll keep my eyes open for that special someone. Trust me, I'd love to meet Mr. Right." She gently pulled her hands back and patted his before picking up the roll of knives. "Until then, a girl's gotta make a living, so I should get going."

"Alright then. Have a great rest of your day." He grinned. "Don't forget to tell all your friends about Bob's Antiques and Collectibles!" he reminded her as she walked out of the shop.

THE FIRST THING MADDY did once back at her place was to get hold of Ashley. She could not believe she had not thought of calling her first, as that was what she usually did when she was stumped by an item. Although her friend mostly dealt with artwork, Bob was right in saying that she might know someone. Maddy was often surprised at how much Ashley knew about the most obscure of objects. Her master's degree certainly had not been wasted on her.

"Hi Maddy," Ashley said. "What's up, buttercup?"

"Umm... what? Who is this, and what have you done with Ashley Muller?"

"Haha, I'm feeling a bit cheeky this afternoon. I closed the deal on that surrealist painting that I told you about. The one that's godawful ugly. I know, I know," Ashley said before Maddy had the chance to interrupt her with her own comments. "I'm always telling you that art is personal, like Spenser's Ducks, and such. But this one? I personally don't get the appeal of that painting! I honestly didn't think it would speak to any of my clients."

"Each to their own, I suppose," Maddy said. "Hey, no matter their taste in art, their money is just as good as the next guy's."

"Very true, thank goodness. Anyway, darling, here I am going on and on about my morning, what about yours? You phoned me, was that to chat or did you have a specific purpose for your call?"

"I have a set of knives I need some help identifying."

"Straight to the point, I like this no-nonsense Maddy! Alrighty then, what kind of knives?"

"That's part of the problem, I'm not sure," Maddy explained. "They look like they're a fancy kitchen set that a chef might use. The knives themselves don't have a name engraved on them, one that's legible anyway, just some kind of marking. The blades are hammered except for the edges. Those are smooth and damn sharp - I slightly cut myself putting them back in - oh, and the case they came in appears to have a signature but, again, I can't make it out. It could only be a squiggly design. I don't even know if the case is original to the knives or not."

"The hammered part makes them sound forged. Those are quality knives. Definitely higher-end, not your average kitchen knife set. That, unfortunately, is about the extent of my knowledge. It doesn't mean that I can't figure this out, though. Hmm..." Ashley went silent for half a beat. "Could be an interesting challenge, that's for sure."

"That's why I thought of you immediately."

"Bob couldn't help you, huh?" Ashley said.

"Yeah, yeah, whatever." Maddy could almost hear Ashley smiling on the other end of the phone. "Can I send you a picture of the knives?"

"You certainly can. If they're high-end knives or knives that belong to a particularly good chef, as I'm suspecting, they could be worth a decent amount. A true professional chef will use one or two sets of knives throughout their career, so they aren't afraid to pay for quality ones. In fact, some will even have knives made by artisans to their specifications."

"I had no idea," Maddy said, surprised.

"Yes, cooking is both science and art to those in the culinary field. They are quite particular about their knives. Some look at them as an extension of their bodies," she added. "Anyway, please take some quick pics of the knives and fire them off to me. You have piqued my interest."

"Okay, hold on a sec." Maddy walked over to the dining room table, where she had left the knife roll. She took a picture of the signature on the leather and then a couple of the knives themselves. She heard the swoosh of the pictures being sent and pressed the phone back to her ear. "You should be getting them any second now," she told Ashley.

Ashley checked the pictures while Maddy waited in silence. Then Maddy heard a rustling noise as her friend seemed to move the phone around.

"I'm just going to look something up online," Ashley said. No other sounds were coming from her end. Maddy was about to ask her what was going on when Ashley finally spoke up.

"It's as I thought. You've hit the jackpot this time, girlfriend!"

"I have?" Maddy sat up. "What did you find out?"

"I'm not 100% sure just yet. They are a quality set and very unique. I think I may have found out who made them. I need to ask someone here in my office to confirm it. How about I do that and get back to you?"

"No problem, I appreciate you looking into it for me," Maddy said. "By the way, did I tell you little Ryan has grown about six inches since the last time Zane and I visited him?"

"Yes, Maddy."

"Oh, well, did I tell you he can fly too, and..."

MADDY WAS PLEASED THAT the knives she had acquired might be worth something. The size of a storage unit didn't matter; only the quality of what was inside did. When she came across something of quality, it would often bring her more profit than if she had a room full of cheap things. She heard a ding come from her phone and picked it up. PopPop had sent her a text.

"Hi Madsy want to do lunch with me at a new joint tomorrow"

"Sounds like fun, I have some errands to run though, might have to be a late lunch." Maddy texted back.

"Why don't I come with you we can visit while you get things done it would be fun love spending time with you" PopPop typed.

"Sounds perfect. You can keep me company! I love spending time with you too, PopPop."

"It's a date then Maddy see you soon can't wait :-)"

Maddy was impressed with PopPop using emojis and texting away like a professional. She smiled, reflecting on how far he had come. Now, she thought, if only she could teach him to use some punctuation. That would be a feat in itself. One step at a time.

Chapter 6

TUESDAY

'I'm not suggesting that you're old and should curl up and wait to die, PopPop. That's not at all what I am getting at," Maddy said as they were cruising with the top down in Bugsy, her yellow Volkswagen Beetle Bug. "I just meant that I don't feel like you have to be doing exhausting things, you've worked hard all your life, and you've earned some relaxation."

"What about my new business venture with George? It's not tiring at all."

"Listen, I'm happy you and George are looking into doing things together and all, nevertheless, please don't overdo it. Keep things simple. Do you really want to start something complicated? Why not join another seniors' club? Maybe start playing Canasta or take some dancing lessons?"

"Are you out of your mind? I already belong to one seniors' club. That's more than enough. They just sit around, drink, play cards, and talk about the good old days. As for dancing, I already know how. They used to call me Randy the Dancing Machine back in the '70s."

"Randy the Dancing Machine?" Maddy giggled, imagining her grandfather doing some disco moves. "Okay, forget about dancing, tell me then what's wrong with sitting around with a drink and passing the time away playing games and chatting? Maybe you could join their board? Suggest other social activities that might interest you more."

"Come on, Maddy. There is no way I can only do stuff with seniors. I may be a senior, but I'm not THAT old. I'm far from being half dead," PopPop was not impressed with her. "George feels the same, by the way. He has millions of dollars and a huge house that anyone would kill for, but he doesn't want to sit around, sip his expensive scotch while watching the world go by. He's just as bored as I am. We both need some real mental stimulation."

"What about some volunteer work?"

PopPop was sitting in the passenger seat, and she could almost sense the side-eye he was giving her.

"Volunteer work? How's that going to keep us stimulated and engaged with life? I mean, we need to be really involved in something interesting."

"Volunteering is stimulating and can be very interesting," she replied. "You'd get to meet lots of people! That would be less stressful than starting up and running your own brand-new business." Maddy couldn't believe her grandfather was considering becoming an entrepreneur at his age. "Please, tell me at least that it's not going to be a large venture like George's other businesses.

"No, it's going to be a small one to start with. It would not make good business sense to go straight into a large affair without testing the waters first," he explained. "Besides, running a small business offers much more than only meeting people! It requires brains and creativity, which I have, and money, which George has to spare," PopPop said. "A business will keep our minds sharp. That's very important as you age, you know."

"Alright, alright, I'll back down, promise." Maddy changed lanes and took a left turn at the lights. "Now, tell me more about it, then. What kind of business?" Maddy had a feeling that nothing she could say or do would dissuade her grandfather.

"We want to cater to seniors in Edmonton and the surrounding area. Did you know that one-fifth of the population in Canada is seniors? We're going to be online too and offer a delivery service. This way we'll be able to reach every single one of them."

"Reach them with what? What are you selling?"

"Edibles for seniors," PopPop said with a wide grin that stretched across the aging face Maddy had always loved.

"Edibles? For seniors? How is that any different from edibles for everyone else?" Maddy asked, trying not to laugh as she carefully backed Bugsy into a parking spot on the street.

"We're going to have all kinds of edibles they want and need. We will particularly focus on the 'need' aspect of it. That will be the biggest difference. Think about it, Maddy. Right now, the most popular edibles available online or in stores are gummies. Do you know what gummies will do to your dentures? Of course you wouldn't. What was I thinking? You're too young." PopPop chuckled. "Well, let me tell you, Maddy, it's not a pretty sight. Imagine snuggling up next to your sweetie pie while sipping a lovely glass of Metamucil-spiked Beaujolais Nouveau. You both pop a gummy to help mellow the mood, and all of a sudden, your dentures are sitting in your lap." He made snapping and sticking sounds with his mouth and made an exaggerated flying denture gesture. "What a way to yuck a guy's yum. It would ruin the mood in a heartbeat!"

Maddy sat in the driver's seat, valiantly trying to get the picture of what her grandfather had described as 'yum' out of her mind. She was unsure which was more disturbing - the dentures on some old geezer's lap or the idea of a man PopPop's age having his yum go to yuck. She sighed. There was no fighting him on this; she might as well find out everything she could about his and George's ideas in case she needed to intervene. At least this way, she could monitor what he was up to and be sure he would not overexert himself. Not that it would matter or make a difference. She sighed again. Then again, one could never tell; maybe they had a gold mine hidden somewhere in this venture of theirs.

"What other kind of edibles will you be offering them?" She had now become a bit invested in her grandfather succeeding and, if she were to be honest, she was more than slightly curious about his and Georges' idea. His talking about it did seem to make him happier and more energetic than before.

"We're still working on what'll be available. At this point, we're thinking apple sauce, scotch mints, bran cereal, tapioca pudding, and a nutritional meal supplement drink," PopPop explained. "Maybe even some kind of infused probiotic drink, too. George thinks we should add cookies and brownies to the menu. I'm not sold on the idea. I think they can get those already. He says we should make it so they can get everything they need in one place. What do you think?"

"Well, he does have a point. People do prefer to get things in one spot. Look at all those mega stores that carry everything from groceries to eyeglasses."

Maddy couldn't believe she was casually having a conversation about cannabis with her grandfather. She was still trying to process the conversation as they pulled into the Triple A parking lot. "You don't want your customers going elsewhere and perhaps not returning. Make it a one-stop shop. You might even attract the younger crowd."

"Hmm, I didn't think of the younger people." PopPop looked thoughtful for a few seconds. He seemed interested in that possibility.

"Think about it," Maddy said. "Their grandkids could bring them to your shop, taste your brownies and scotch mints, maybe even try a smoothie. Then they would come back with their friends. Why stop at mints? Hard caramels, lemon drops. Perhaps even Nanaimo bars and butter tarts too!"

"Oooh! Look at that creative business brain of yours! Maybe we should bring you on board as an advisor, what do you think?"

"I'm not so sure. I'm not that knowledgeable in the subject matter. Cannabis isn't my thing, I prefer a good glass of wine to unwind."

Maddy expected some kind of response or reaction from her grandfather, however, he seemed focused on something else.

"What do we have to do here?" he asked, staring over her shoulder.

"I want to grab a box out of my unit." She turned to look at what had caught his eye. Maddy saw nothing unusual that might have attracted anyone's attention and turned back to face him. "It shouldn't take long. We'll have plenty of quality time for lunch, don't worry."

"Don't rush on my account, I have all the time in the world to spend with you, Mads. We don't get to do this nearly enough," he said.

They were walking across the lot when Rod and his aunt Shirley came flying out of the office, her floral caftan flapping in the wind.

"Maddy! Maddy!" She threw her arms around Maddy, almost knocking her off her feet. "Rod told me how much you helped him while I was gone. I can't thank you enough."

"I didn't do anything, honestly," she said.

"So humble!" Aunt Shirley swatted at Maddy's arm hard enough that she would probably wake up with a nasty bruise the next morning.

"Well, well, well, who do we have here?" PopPop's voice sounded deeper than usual.

"You can call me Aunt Shirley, everybody around here does," she said, looking him up and down like he was a slice of chocolate cake. Then she presented him with her hand held loosely out. PopPop placed it in his, still smiling at her.

"You are much too beautiful for me to think of you as my aunt," he said, winking at her.

Maddy stared at them in disbelief, not certain about what she was watching unfold in front of her eyes, an odd feeling of dread forming in the pit of her stomach.

PopPop bent over and placed a kiss on her hand. His lips lingered longer than necessary. This caused Aunt Shirley to elicit a strange laugh that Maddy would later describe to her friends as a mix of a giggle and a twitter. "Maddy, you didn't tell me you were acquainted with such a charming and handsome gentleman."

"This is PopPop, Aunt Shirley, he's my grandfather. We lost touch years ago when I was little. We found each other again while you were living in Hawaii." Maddy didn't bother explaining that he was her step-grandfather, nor that her family had falsely claimed that her beloved PopPop had died.

"Well, PopPop, I'm very pleased to meet you," she replied, her eyes never leaving his.

"You can call me Randall," he said, still holding onto her hand.

Maddy had the uncomfortable feeling that she was witnessing firsthand what PopPop had meant when he had referred to his 'Yum'.

"Maybe once I get to know you a little better, I'll be able to call you Randy," Aunt Shirley said, looking at PopPop from under fluttering eyelashes, a sly smile on her brightly frosted pink lips.

"I look forward to that day," PopPop raised both his eyebrows in response.

'*This cannot be happening*!' Maddy thought to herself. '*I feel like I'm in a Twilight Zone episode rerun.*'

Aunt Shirley and PopPop were in their very own world, completely ignoring Rod and Maddy. Rod looked at Maddy, confusion written all over his face. She replied by shrugging her shoulders.

"It was nice to see you again, Aunt Shirley," Maddy said. "We're just on our way to pick up a box from my unit. PopPop, you were going to give me a hand with it?"

"I can do that," Rod spoke up quickly. "I can help."

"Oh, I don't..." She looked over at PopPop. They still were paying her absolutely no attention and did not even appear to have heard her. "Okay, Rod, let's go."

Rod pushed his combover out of his face and patted his hair down, trying to keep it in place. He stood as tall as his five feet would allow him and followed behind her, taking two strides for every one of hers.

Maddy was deep in thought and did not notice. All she could think of was this new starstruck duo of Aunt Shirley and PopPop. What happened to Bob? And why was PopPop so taken with the muumuu-wearing, glittery lipsticked Aunt Shirley? She shivered at the thought of the two of them together. It was not because Shirley was a terrible woman; on the contrary, Maddy quite liked her eccentric personality. She was more concerned about the 'Yum' sparkle that was shining in both of their eyes. That could only mean a boatload of trouble for them, poor Bob, and not the least for her. She knew she would end up right smack in the middle of a love triangle.

WITH THE BOX OF ITEMS she needed safely tucked away in Bugsy's trunk, Maddy pried her grandfather out of Aunt Shirley's flirty hands and placed him in the passenger seat of the car. They left the Triple A and headed to one of Maddy's clients' workplace. She needed to pick up a cheque for some items he had purchased.

"I can't believe you held out on me," PopPop said. "What a lovely lady Rod's aunt Shirley is."

"Uh-hmmm..." Maddy said. "You know she and Bob, from Bernard's, are a couple."

"Pfft! I don't mind a little competition; it just makes the win that much sweeter."

They spent the rest of the afternoon driving around Edmonton, picking up and dropping off items. Maddy was enjoying his company. It beat spending the day alone.

"Thanks for coming along with me on my errands this morning," she glanced over at him while they were stopped at a red traffic light. He was beaming. "I love our time together."

"I'm so happy that I saw your listing for that one-dollar loonie on Marketplace," he told her. "I never would have imagined in a million years that a one-dollar duck coin would have brought us back to each other."

"You know, PopPop, having you back in my life filled an empty space in my heart that I didn't know was there."

"I know what you mean, sweetheart. I feel the same way.

One less empty spot in my heart to fill."

Maddy looked at him again, he looked like his mind had wandered to some other time. His expression was one of deep loneliness. Right then, she understood how he felt. He was looking for a different companionship, one she couldn't provide him with.

"Food! I need food!" she exclaimed loudly, nudging him out of his reverie. "How do you feel about Greek?"

"If you're referring to food and not the language, then OPA! I'm all in." PopPop smiled and gave her a thumbs-up.

She had succeeded in distracting him.

They settled on Yiannis, a popular Greek taverna on Whyte Avenue. Sitting down at a table by the window, they dug into their lunch with great appetite.

"I hadn't realized how hungry I was. Great suggestion, Maddy. It's the first time I've ever eaten here." PopPop said, dipping his forkful of calamari into a small dish filled with tzatziki sauce.

"It's one of the best. I've been coming here forever," she said, stabbing a slice of cucumber sprinkled with feta cheese nestled deep in her large bowl of Greek salad. "Ashley introduced it to me while in her first year of university."

"Did she now?"

"Yup!"

"That lovely friend of yours has good taste."

"Did you see that Mexican restaurant next door?"

"I sure did. It looks fun and lively. Might want to go there one day."

"It is. It's pretty loud at night and usually filled with university students, so it's best for you to go during the daytime." She laughed. "That's where Ash, Rick, and I met Tasha for the first time."

"I bet Rick was smitten from the get-go."

"He sure was. There was no going back for those two. They fell hard for each other."

"There's nothing like meeting someone and falling for them at first sight. Nothing like it at all." There was that lonely look on his face again. Then, something seemed to have crossed his mind, and he suddenly cheered up and asked, "How long has Shirley been with Bob?"

"They met when they were both in Hawaii," she said. She didn't elaborate further, hoping to quickly change the subject. "How far have you and George gotten in planning your edibles store?" Talking about the edibles shop was a far safer topic of conversation, at least in Maddy's opinion.

"We've finished our business plan and now we're trying to decide on a name and find a location," he answered.

"Do you have a list of potential names yet?" A grin spread over PopPop's face.

"We certainly do! Maybe you can help us. I know you aren't a senior, still, I would love your feedback."

"Of course, I'd be more than happy to," she said, pleased to have distracted him from the Aunt Shirley subject. "Fire away."

"We have a few on the short list. We like 'Puff 'n Pensioners' best, but because they are edibles and not smokes, it isn't a perfect fit. Then there is 'Grandpa's Ganja', that's a contender for me. George is kinda stuck on 'High Time for Seniors'. What do you think?" he asked.

Maddy had to give them some credit; George and PopPop were pretty creative with coming up with store names. They were a tad odd, yet were creative nonetheless.

"Umm... like you said, I'm not a senior, so I'm not sure I'm the best person to ask."

"I know, sweetheart, I value your opinion, though. You are a very creative-minded person when it comes to business," PopPop said.

"Okay, well, some seniors may not be familiar with the word ganja, although I do like the alliteration. You already pointed out the issue with 'Puff 'n Pensioners'. I like the 'High Time' one, although it is rather on the nose about it being for seniors."

"I was thinking that too, then it's clear who the store is for," he explained. "I like alliterations. We need to find just the right one, and by the way, we North American seniors know what ganja is. The word is older than me. It's Indian, but Jamaicans are the ones who made its use popular. Your generation didn't come up with everything, you know, young lady?"

Maddy was not sure that this topic of conversation was any better than Aunt Shirley was. PopPop's apparent in-depth knowledge of marijuana was a tad disturbing. In life, there are certain things a grandchild does not need or want to know about their grandparents - their sex lives and recreational drug use being at the top of that list.

TUESDAY

THIS IS DAMN GOOD SPAGHETTI' Maddy thought. *'I wish I had time to make myself some home-cooked meals more often.'* Maddy didn't have a lot of recipes in her cooking repertoire, but her spaghetti sauce from scratch was one of her best. To be honest, even if she had had an extra hour or two in her day, she would not use them to cook. Spending time in the kitchen was far from being her favorite activity. Although occasionally, she did enjoy playing Suzy Homemaker. This evening happened to be one of them. As she was helping herself to another plateful, her cell buzzed on the dining room table. She placed her second serving down and sat before looking at the screen to see who was interrupting her dinner. Maddy didn't like to talk to people during her 'me' time, unless it was Ashley, Rick, or Tasha. If she didn't answer them, they would keep calling until she did. Especially Ashley, who was a worrier when it came to Maddy, and with good cause, as she had proven to her over the years.

"Hey Ash."

"Good evening, Mads. I know it's suppertime, but I found out some exciting news about those knives of yours!" Ashley sounded unusually enthusiastic. "I couldn't wait to share it with you."

"Really?" Maddy felt her heart rate increase from excitement. "Don't hold back, tell me, tell me!"

"I asked around the office and found out that your knives should probably go in an international auction. The clientele for them is small, however, they are willing to pay generously for such items."

"I like the sounds of that," Maddy said.

"I thought you might," Ashley laughed. "One of the knives is a Japanese quail carving knife. A Masashi Kuroshu Honesuki knife, to be precise. This particular set was owned by a long-deceased and well-renowned Japanese chef. That increases the set's value."

"Oooh, that sounds very promising! Is this sale something you can help me with?" Maddy was delighted by the news.

"Of course. I'm sorry, though, I'll need to take a percentage of the sale as commission for the company," Ashley explained. "I can't get around that, but I won't charge you my fee."

"Aww, thanks, hon, I appreciate that, and I completely understand about the company commission. I'm just happy that they might be worth something!"

"Thanks for understanding. I'll prepare some agreement forms for you to sign. We'll also need to get some good photos of the knives," Ashley added. "Could you come into the office tomorrow sometime?"

"Does three in the afternoon work for you?"

"Yes, I'm free then. Let me put it in my work calendar." Ashley made some tapping sounds on her cellphone. There, done. See you at three."

"You betcha!"

Maddy spent the rest of the evening revising a special budget she had been working on. She had prepared a spreadsheet that laid out what she needed brick-and-mortar store. Depending on how much the knives would bring, she was happily getting closer to her goal. Her dream was coming within sight, she could almost touch it.

WEDNESDAY

"BUONGIORNO BELLA!" Tasha's happy voice greeted Maddy on the other end of the line.

"Well, good morning to you, too, Tash!" She never got tired of hearing her friend speak Italian to her. As a result, she had managed to pick up a few words herself along the way. "What can I do for you, my 'bella' friend?"

"Look at you speaking Italian right back to me! You have no idea how happy it makes me."

"I have a strong suspicion. What I would like to know is why you're up so early on your day off ?"

"I received a call from the restaurant where I had the interview. They want me to come in for a trial run!" Tasha replied. She had been out of work for months now. "Anyway, I can't talk for long. The girls received the vintage clothes you sent them. They loved every single one of them. Thank you!"

"Did they, really?"

"Yes, I swear. Chloe even squealed when she saw those flowery bellbottoms. They fit her perfectly."

"That makes me so happy. I love spoiling my goddaughters."

"And they love being spoiled by you," Tasha replied. "You can expect a thank-you call from them this week."

"That's not necessary."

"It most certainly is! Anyway, I have to jump in the shower. Brunch at our place on Sunday, don't forget. Have a wonderful day. Ciao!"

"Sounds good... You too!" Maddy laughed at Tasha's quick conversations. The woman never wasted time telling you what she wanted. It was one thing she appreciated about her - nice short conversations. Which was a good thing too, as Maddy had a lot to squeeze in her day before meeting Ashley in the afternoon.

TRYING TO PARK IN THE lot closest to Ashley's downtown office was always challenging. Forget about using the parkade garage below it; that was even worse. Maddy looked up at the imposing office tower as she walked toward it. Whenever she visited Ashley here, she could not help but think of how different and far away this world seemed from the one they grew up in. They never would have imagined that Ashley would not only work in a fancy building like this, but that she would also have a large corner office near the top.

What about her? Was her life what she had imagined it to be? She pondered that thought as she waited for the elevator. Maddy couldn't remember what she thought back then. Always going with the flow had been her preference because chances were, if you did not, you would be fighting a losing battle. One thing she had certainly never thought about was how her three friends would end up being like family. Truth be told, closer than family. Maddy's had not exactly been the epitome of a nice, average family. She had an emotionally abusive stepfather. Her mother, although very loving, had fought cancer and been in and out of hospitals for almost all of Maddy's adolescent years. PopPop was the only person she was still in contact with these days, and that was by pure serendipity.

"Hi, I'm here to see Ashley Mueller," Maddy told the receptionist. It seemed like they had a different one every time she came to visit. "She's expecting me."

"Just one moment, please."

Maddy stood waiting, clasping the knife roll close to her chest. Knowing they might be worth a lot of money, she was feeling a bit nervous and paranoid about carrying them around. She wished that she had put them in a carrying case or purse.

"Hello Maddy, come in," Ashley said from the doorway to the right of the receptionist. "Thanks, Alyssa."

"Yes, thank you." Maddy smiled at the receptionist. Being the new kid on the block was never easy, so she made sure to acknowledge Alyssa and not act as if she didn't exist. She walked back with Ashley to her office where a man in an impeccably tailored navy-blue suit and a light pink shimmery tie was waiting for them. She was no connoisseur of men's suits, nonetheless, it was obvious the man's outfit was worth more than her monthly rent.

"Maddy, let me introduce you to my colleague, Joshua Hampton. He is our resident knife specialist," Ashley said with a smile. "Josh, this is my friend, Maddy Whitman."

"Pleasure to meet you, Maddy," Joshua reached out and shook her hand.

"The pleasure is all mine." Maddy immediately noticed his eyes. They were a striking light blue, almost grey. A scent she couldn't quite place wafted off him and tickled her nose. She loved a man who wore aftershave. Too bad there were fewer of them these days, she thought.

"I hear you have come into possession of some unique knives," he said.

"I'm hoping so," Maddy said. "They're in here." She passed him the roll. He placed them on Ashley's table and then donned some white cotton gloves before unrolling the knives. Picking up one of them, he looked closely at the handle. Then he turned it over and looked at the other side. After scrutinizing it, he turned his attention to the blade. He laid the knife down and picked up the next one in the roll and repeated the process. He did that with every knife in the roll before finally rolling it back up and taking off his gloves with an air of satisfaction.

"Well?" Ashley had been quiet throughout the whole process, and could no longer wait to hear his expert opinion.

"You were absolutely right, these are exactly what we thought," Joshua said, a grin spreading on his face. "The original owner was a man from Japan who was well known in his time as one of the best 'Itamae' in the country."

"What's an 'Itamae'?" Maddy asked.

"That would be the equivalent of 'Master Chef' in Japan."

"How very cool," Ashley said, bending over to admire them.

"Oh, but there's more." Joshua looked impressed. "They passed through only a few talented hands after his death, finally ending up with a Canadian chef who studied and worked in Paris. He left Europe and returned home to Canada in total disgrace. Many angry creditors are looking high and low for him. Last I heard, he was still alive. I don't think he's working any longer, at least nowhere credible. No one wants to touch him as he is quite unreliable. He has a major problem with alcohol, gambling, is extremely temperamental, and has a penchant for expensive items..." He pointed to the roll on top of Ashley's desk. "Such as very expensive knives."

"How much do you think they could be worth?" Maddy asked and held her breath, praying to hear a large sum in reply.

"Well, like anything similar to these, it isn't so much what they're worth, it's more like what people are willing to pay for them," Joshua explained. "We need to put them in the right auction and then spread the word to our networks about the collection. Hopefully, it will fall into the ears of at least two buyers with big pockets."

"Two buyers?" Maddy asked.

"Yes, one to bid it up and the other to buy it," Joshua said with a smile. "I would be greatly disappointed if they brought in less than $10,000. Especially with the vintage Honesuki quail carving knife as part of the set. The knives alone aren't what would bring in top dollar. It's the story behind them and their original owner. That's why we need to put them in a special auction. Stories sell. The stranger and more unique the history attached to an object, the more collectors desire it."

"Wow, that would be amazing," Maddy said as she sat down in the chair near the table. "When will it be in the auction?"

"I'm still doing some research on that," Ashley joined her at the table. "Joshua has given me some suggestions, and I'm going to look into them to make sure they have the clientele we need. In the meantime, we need to start spreading the word about the collection."

"Okay, sounds good. Is there anything I need to do?" Maddy asked them both.

"Nope, leave everything to us. I'll have professional photos taken so when we decide on an auction, we will be ready to list them," Ashley said.

"Well, that's easy." Maddy laughed.

"Thank you for your help, Josh," Ashley said as he readied himself to leave her office.

"Yes, thank you very much, Joshua." Maddy stood up and shook his hand goodbye.

"No problem at all, Ashley. It was my pleasure to meet you, Maddy, and see those knives in person."

After Joshua left the room, Maddy turned to Ashley. "Why haven't I heard about this Mr. Hampton before, girlfriend? Are you holding out on me?"

"Not at all," Ashley said. "He's taken."

"Oh rats! That's such a shame."

"His husband doesn't think so."

"I need to find myself a Joshua without a partner."

"You most definitely do."

Chapter 7

FRIDAY

"Thanks for coming to help me again, Rick. I need to temporarily move some of my things to my place until Rod repairs part of the damage done to the walls inside my unit."

"That lumberjack guy did a heck of a number on it, eh?"

"Yeah, it turns out that some of the things that dipshidiot smashed against the walls damaged them. Go figure."

"No worries, let's start putting the boxes in my truck, then we'll move the stuff that's not going anywhere to the middle of the locker so Rod can get around them more easily."

They spent some time reorganizing all her belongings. One trunk was too valuable to leave behind while workers were fixing her unit. It was too big to move to her apartment. They were discussing what to do when Rod showed up.

"Hey guys, do you need any help?"

"As a matter of fact, I do, Rod." She gave him one of her sweetest smiles. "Can I store this trunk and its contents in your office, please?"

"Sure, we can put it in the back room. We're using it to store some of Aunt Shirley's extra furniture. There's a mattress, a couple of boxes of her collectibles that her ex didn't know about, stuff like that. I don't think she'd mind," Rod replied.

"Let me give you a hand with it, Rod, it's kinda heavy," Rick said as he lifted one end. Rod bent down to take the other.

Maddy watched them walk away. Rick was now the one bending over, and Rod had his arms uncomfortably above his waist. They made quite the comical pair. Once they were out of view, she went back to transferring some of the smaller items that were left into Rick's truck. She was surprised to hear the two guys coming back already. Rod was swearing, Rick was laughing hysterically. This was unusual. Rod didn't swear often, and his sense of humor wasn't particularly the kind to send anyone into fits of laughter. She walked back to the locker's entrance and saw them returning with the trunk. They were awkwardly running back with it.

"What's going on? Why are you guys bringing the trunk back? Was there no room for it?"

"Oh, there was room for it, alright. Unfortunately, the space is otherwise occupied." Rick guffawed as they put the trunk down.

"What are you talking about, Rick?" Maddy had no idea what was so funny. "Why are you laughing?"

"Oh, he thinks what we saw is hilarious, but not I. No, certainly not I!" Rod answered. "What if it was your mother or aunt in there, 'Mister-this-is-SO-funny', eh?"

"Don't you even dare bring my mama into this conversation!" Rick immediately stopped laughing. His face turned a shade of red.

"Not so funny now, hmm?" Rod poked him in the shoulder. Rick shrugged him off.

"Would one of you please tell me what's going on?" Maddy couldn't follow their dizzying back-and-forth argument. "And what does Mama Leila have to do with any of this? Or anyone's mother for that matter?"

"She has nothing to do with this, NOTHING!" Rick said adamantly. "It's all about his aunt and your Romeo of a grandfather."

"PopPop? What has he gotten into this time?"

Maddy's question made Rick burst into laughter once again. Rod was fuming and giving him a dirty look.

"'Who', not 'what'." Rick sputtered out, unable to stop laughing.

"THAT'S not funny! It's downright damn disrespectful, Rick. Stop it right this damn minute! Stop being a jerk!" Rod was fit to be tied.

"I'm sorry, Rod, you're right. It's very disrespectful." Rick truly looked apologetic. "It's just that now I have hope for the future. A lot of hope."

"Yeah, there's that. I can't argue with you here." Rod's attitude seemed to change, and he smiled sheepishly at Rick. "But now I'm scarred for life. That image is forever burned in my brain."

"It was not a pretty sight, man, I'll admit that." Rick shook his head.

"Will one of you PLEASE tell me what's going on?" Maddy was so upset she stomped her foot, making both men stare at her as if she had lost her mind.

"Alright, prepare yourself not to like what I'm about to tell you," Rick replied.

"I. Don't. Care!" Maddy exclaimed. "Spit it out. NOW!"

"Rod opened the door to the back room and..." Rick started laughing once more. "I...can't... I can't..." he stammered out of breath. "Rod... you tell... her." He could no longer control himself.

"There was SO much white wrinkly skin, and it was moving in ways I've never seen old skin move." As soon as these words came out of his mouth, Rod realized what he had said. It was now his turn to lose all control. He couldn't help but start laughing hysterically; tears were running down his cheeks. This only encouraged Rick, who by now had completely lost it. He was bent over in painful laughter, unable to catch his breath.

Maddy was trying to make sense of what they were saying. PopPop was getting into trouble with someone, something was in the way of putting the trunk in the room, old white skin, disrespectful, not Mama Leila ... Her eyes grew wide. Slowly, it had begun to dawn on her.

"Maddy! Rod! Please, we can explain!" Aunt Shirley was yelling as she and PopPop were walking toward her locker as fast as their old legs could carry them. PopPop was trying to shove his shirt into his pants while Aunt Shirley was wiggling around in her caftan.

"OH LORD NO! NO! NO!" Maddy's worst nightmare was hobbling at full speed in her direction. She wanted nothing to do with it. She turned to the guys and gave them both the dirtiest of looks. "How can you both be standing here laughing?"

"We're not, Maddy, not really. It's shock!" Rick said. "It's hard on one's mind when you walk in on people in 'flagrante delicto', you know."

"Yeah, it was fragrant delicio... or whatever he said. I'm...I'm scarred for life!" Rod added.

"Madsy, please let me explain," PopPop said while huffing and puffing. "It's not what it looks like."

"Randy, it kind of is," Aunt Shirley corrected him. "Well, yes, Shirl is right, but still..." PopPop continued.

"Nope, she called you 'Randy'. I don't want to hear it. I don't want to know about it. I don't even want to imagine it!" Maddy covered her ears and walked toward Rick's truck. "Rick, take me home, now. Rod, please lock my unit up on your way out."

"You got it, Maddy," Rod replied.

Rick slowly made his way to the truck, stopping to pat PopPop on the back. "Way to go, old guy, way to go."

"NOW, Rick!" Maddy demanded through the truck's open window.

SATURDAY

"MADDY WHITMAN?" A WELL-dressed older woman asked as she drew near to the cafe table Maddy was sitting at.

"Yes, and you must be Jacqueline Stefanos?" The woman nodded, and Maddy invited her to sit down on the chair across from her.

Thank you for meeting me here at Vi's," Jacqueline said. "I know it's a bit hard to get to with all the construction on Stony Plain Road, but it's a walkable distance for me. My car is at the mechanic's today."

"Oh, no worries at all," Maddy said. "I love their selection of pies and cakes."

"They are divine, aren't they?"

"Here's the Royal Crown Derby platter." She pulled it out of a bag and handed her the piece of wrapped china. "You'll notice that it's in excellent condition. No scratches or chips."

Jacqueline unwrapped it and turned it around, inspecting it closely. "It's beautiful! Look at how the colors are not faded at all. It will be a perfect addition to my collection, thank you."

"It's my pleasure. I love finding objects that bring joy to others. It's my true passion, finding a treasure and then someone who will cherish it."

"You can rest assured that I will cherish this piece!" Jacqueline rewrapped the platter and put it in the bag Maddy handed her.

"Is it the china pattern that attracted you, or did you inherit it from a relative?" Maddy always liked to find out the stories behind why her clients purchased an object from her.

"Yes and no. I don't care so much about the pattern as about the memories it brings me." Jacqueline looked thoughtful for a moment, then continued. "My grandmother used to serve our special family dinners on this service. I was the only granddaughter, and she left it to me."

"How lovely!" Maddy enjoyed hearing this. She never knew either of her grandmothers. "You're adding to the set with this, then?"

"No, I'm actually rebuilding my set. We had a fire while we were renovating. Our dining room was the only room that was damaged by fire, thankfully. Unfortunately, it was totally destroyed. My granny Maureen's china, along with the buffet it was displayed in, were a burnt mess."

"Oh no, I'm so sorry to hear that. You must have been devastated." What a sad story, Maddy thought.

"Thank you. Yes, it was heartbreaking for me. Then my husband had the great idea of using the insurance money to start a treasure hunt in her honor. Now I'm always on the lookout for rare pieces. Every time I search for any Royal Crown Derby chinaware, I think of her. When I find one, it's as if Granny is looking down on me and gifting me the china all over again."

"That's such a lovely way of looking at it." This story was wonderful after all. What a beautiful ending. "Do you have the salt and pepper shakers set by any chance?"

"No. I have a feeling, however, that you do." Jacqueline's eyes twinkled with joy.

"As a matter of fact, I do." Maddy smiled back at her and pulled them out of another bag. She was glad to have brought them along. Sometimes she followed her instincts. They weren't always right. This time, it had paid off to listen to them. To say that Jacqueline was pleased would have been an understatement. She left as happy as can be with both the platter and the shakers in her possession. Maddy sat back, filled with a fuzzy, warm feeling and a fuller wallet. Now, if she could manage to hold on to that warm fuzziness until PopPop showed up. He had begged her to meet for coffee and explain things. She dreaded hearing his explanation. Saying no to meeting him was not something she could do, nor was staying upset with him. She loved him too much for that.

"Why are seniors so frustrating?" she asked herself out loud.

"Because we don't want to be treated like infants while we still have all of our senses, that's why, sweetheart," her grandfather replied as he came from behind her and sat down.

"Oh, PopPop, you weren't supposed to hear that."

"Then you shouldn't have said it with your outside voice." He squeezed her hand. "I'm sorry if I've become a cause of stress to you."

"Never say that, please." Maddy squeezed his hand back. "You'll never become a bother, and you don't cause me stress."

He gave her one of those knowing looks.

"Okay, perhaps a tiny bit of stress," she acknowledged with a grin. "Please, put yourself in my place, PopPop. Bob is a friend of mine and someone I depend on for my business. He's always buying stuff from me. Not only that," she added, "he teaches me invaluable things about antiques."

"I know that, sweetheart. I appreciate all the help he has been giving you." He patted her hand.

"Then why are you endangering my relationship with him?" she asked. "Are you that taken with Rod's aunt Shirley?"

"Well, I have to admit that I am quite smitten with that love muffin of a woman..."

"Please, don't call her that in front of me." Maddy cut him off.

"Okay, no pet names in front of you." PopPop chuckled. "Please, either convince Shirley to call it off with Bob or stop seeing her. Bob is so in love, I can't bear to see him hurt," Maddy explained. "And certainly not by my very own grandfather." PopPop looked at the obvious distress on his granddaughter's face.

"Okay, Madsy, you're right. I'll talk to Shirl and take care of this."

"Thank you."

"Anything for you, my Madsy." He patted her hand. "And anyway, you're right, it's only proper that we do this above board so we don't hurt people unnecessarily. I guess I just got caught up in feeling things I didn't know I could feel again."

"Nope, don't wanna hear it." Maddy held up her palms facing him.

"I mean, feeling these emotions, Maddy," PopPop laughed out loud at her discomfort.

There was a brief silence before Maddy decided to change the topic.

"How are plans coming along for your new business venture?" she asked.

"Good, we have a line on the perfect space, located in the perfect area," PopPop grinned with pleasure. "And we have decided on a name."

"Really, what is it?"

"Now, before I tell you, I need to say that if you don't like it, please don't tell me. We're really happy with this name, and it is what my partner George and I have decided it is going to be called."

"Okay, I promise," Maddy said.

"The name of the store is 'Half-Baked' and then in smaller print it will say 'for seniors,'" he said happily. "We figured with a bakery on site, it was the perfect name!"

"Oh, I do like it, PopPop!" Maddy enthused. "And the double meaning is so cute!"

"What do you mean by double meaning?" He frowned and looked confused.

"Umm... well, with the name... it refers to the bakery but also... umm..." Maddy floundered, unsure how to explain it to her grandpa. "The bakery meaning, of course. Half-baked in the cannabis or marijuana culture, though, means to be..."

She looked away and was searching for the right word. Maddy turned back toward her grandfather and saw that PopPop was having a hard time holding in his laughter.

"Oh, you!" Sqhe batted at his arm. "Stop with all the teasing. I never know when you're being serious anymore."

"That was too much fun!" His shoulders shook from laughter. "The look on your face as you tried to describe 'half-baked' to your elderly grandfather!"

"Why do you have to be so mean to me?" Maddy asked, a smile on her face.

"The same reason why you insist that your generation invented everything from sex to marijuana!"

"Fair enough," Maddy shook her head at him. "But I'm not going to forget it. I'll get back at you when you least expect it..."

"I'll probably deserve it." His amusement made his eyes twinkle. "I just about forgot - how are the plans for a real shop going? Did that break-in put you behind?"

"I'm not sure quite yet," Maddy said. "The insurance is looking into it and should give me a call sometime by the end of the week, which is tomorrow."

"Hopefully they won't give you too hard a time." He looked at her, then added, "If you need a loan or anything, please ask me, okay?"

"Thank you." His offer meant a lot. It was nice to know she could depend on at least one relative. "I want to try to do this on my own if I can. I need to prove it to myself."

"I completely understand. I don't think I've ever told you this, but I am very proud of the woman you've become. Especially that you did it all on your own."

"To be honest, PopPop, I owe a great deal of gratitude to Rick's parents. His mom, in particular. Mama Leila is a wonderful person with the biggest heart imaginable."

"I'd love to meet her one day, she sounds lovely," he said. "Now, let's order some pie, I am famished!"

Chapter 8

SUNDAY

"Are you ready to head off to your car show?" Maddy asked Rick. "Must be rough to have to go to Vegas for it."

"He keeps telling me it's a burden he must bear," Tasha groaned. "He goes on and on and on about how he hates flying and how the session on emerging trends is so far from the one on electric car repairs, which is further yet from the car kit one that in the end he's going to be sooo exhausted."

"Poor baby!" Ashley chimed in. "We feel for you having to spend such a long time in Las Vegas."

"Yeah, pools, sponsors' parties, swag bags... that does sound very draining." Maddy winked at him.

"I feel rather ganged up on here," Rick said. "It's not just a car show. There are sessions for industry professionals as well. Shop owners, dealership owners, etc. You have no idea what it's like, surrounded by people who live and breathe auto body repair. You think that I go on and on, Tasha? You haven't heard those people go on and on, it's non-stop. It's truly too much."

Maddy threw a couch pillow at him, having regularly accused Rick of doing the same thing. He was passionate about his work, dedicated to every aspect, down to the last detail. That is what made his body shop so successful and his customers loyal.

"How are you going to pass the time with the hubby gone?" Ashley turned toward Tasha.

"I thought I was going to have all this me time, then I started a new job on Thursday and...." Tasha sighed. "I was looking forward to some time without Rick or the girls, but that job is too good to pass up."

"What? I thought you were waiting for the funeral home to reopen?" Ashley asked.

"You didn't know that, Ash?" Maddy smiled like a Cheshire cat. She loved knowing stuff before Ashley did.

"I did not!' She gave Maddy a dirty look. "Spill the details, Tasha."

"I was waiting, then this opportunity came up and, Dio mio, I'm tired of waiting for them to call me back to work. Last time I talked to my boss, she said the whole project had been caught up in red tape or something," Tasha said. "Again."

"Or crime scene tape," Ashley laughed.

"Tsk, no, that's been removed a long time ago," Tasha replied, waving her hand. The demolished funeral home where Tasha used to work was where they saved a woman from dying at the hands of a crazed serial killer and barely got away with their own lives. "First, the problem had to do with permits. Then, they needed new cremation chambers or something like that," she said. "You know, those ovens they put the bodies in? She wanted deeper ones because people now are longer or taller, whichever, so they fit better."

"Oh gawd!" Maddy tried not to giggle.

"There's always something to slow things down. I can't wait forever after her," Tasha griped.

"Seriously, though, that's great news, Tasha." Ashley was quite happy for her and wanted to know more about this new job. "Where exactly are you working and what will you be doing?"

"It's a hostess position at a new French restaurant on 118th Avenue. I haven't worked in a restaurant since I was in high school. Since I was kind of a hostess at the funeral home and dealt with all sorts of emotional people, they thought I could handle a restaurant crowd. Anyway, it pays well, the tips so far have been fantastic, and the staff is so much fun. My manager lets me set my schedule so that I'm home when the girls leave and come home from school, that's what's most important for me. I can even start after Rick gets home for evening shifts. Rick's mom said she'd also help while Rick's away or if he has to work late. Plus, the food is to die for!"

"That's awesome, Tasha!" Ashley said.

A voice from the kitchen piped up, "We don't need anyone to look after us anymore. We're teenagers, not some little kids!"

"It's rude to eavesdrop, Chloe! Aren't you supposed to be cleaning your room?" Rick hollered back.

"I finished."

"Don't you have an assignment due tomorrow?"

"Yeah..."

"Then get at it!"

"Yes, daaad."

"Yes, what??"

"Ugh! Yes, Baba," Chloe mumbled as they heard her stomp up the stairs.

"I don't remember ever being that whiny," Rick said.

"Ha!" Maddy looked at him, grinning.

"Were you, Tasha?" Rick asked, ignoring Maddy.

"As a teenager? Absolutely, amore mio," she laughed.

"I'm sorry, Rick, I can't sit here and let you deny your teenage whininess." Maddy started laughing. "Have you forgotten, I lived with you and your family from grade 11 onward?"

"I concur with Maddy. You were quite whiny," Ashley said, adding her two cents' worth.

"I was not whiny! I objected to certain house rules. That's all. What's with everybody today? All of you, stop picking on me!"

Tasha couldn't stop laughing. "What's new for you, Maddy?" she asked, changing the subject before her husband started pouting.

"Well, Ryan is getting ready to be released, and we're a bit nervous about that. I still think of him as a wee little gosling."

"We?" Rick asked, cocking one eyebrow.

"Yes, wee as in small," She was getting a bit tired of this constant badgering from her friends about her relationship with Zane.

"Not wee, 'we.'"

This time, Rick used air quotes. "Oh! Why didn't you say so? 'We' is Zane and I."

"You've been spending a lot of time with Zane lately," Rick commented. "Are you sure there isn't more you want to tell us?"

"Yes, I'm sure. Zane and I are just friends," Maddy said. "Don't you start on me, too. As I already told Tasha, we've been spending time together because of Ryan, that's it, that's all."

"So, you two decided to stay together for the kid's sake?" Ashley teased. "What about that contest or game or whatever it was that you were playing with him around the time you two adopted Ryan?"

"That was just something he found in one of his auction lots; he needed my help," Maddy said. "We'd hoped we would win a year's supply of... something, but it didn't work out."

"Are you sure he views things the same way?" Rick asked. "I've only met him a couple of times, and he seems like a nice guy. I'd hate to see him hoping for one thing and you another."

"I'm sure he knows. We treat each other like friends, nothing more. There is no romance there, none whatsoever. Zero."

"Maybe not. Maddy, you have to be clear with him just in case. We guys can be a bit dumb and also blind when we like someone. Don't lead him on by mistake."

"Point taken," Maddy said, then quickly changed the subject. "The other interesting thing is that I found some knives in a lot I won at one of the auctions. Turns out they're worth a nice little sum. Ashley's going to put them in an international auction to get the most cashola for them."

"Oooh, that's wonderful!" Tasha said. "That should help with your store fund, right?"

"Absolutely, just keep your fingers crossed that the auction goes well."

"What kind of knives are they that they are worth so much?" Tasha asked.

"Some kind of chef's knives made in Japan. They have quite a story behind them. Who knew knives could have such interesting histories?"

Tasha suddenly sat up straight in her chair and snapped her fingers. "I have an idea!"

"What?" Maddy asked, surprised at her sudden exclamation.

"Maybe the chef at my restaurant would be interested in the knives, I could ask him."

Maddy exchanged looks with Ashley. They appeared to be thinking the same thing.

"I don't think you understand, Tasha, they're worth a lot of money," Ashley said. "Big bucks, like over $10,000."

"Yeah, I get it. So what?" Tasha looked from Maddy to Ashley, a frown marring her face.

"I'm not sure that a chef from a restaurant in Edmonton would be looking for knives of that caliber," Maddy said.

"Oh, really?" Tasha elongated the 'really' and squinted her eyes at them.

"*Uh oh, they had pissed Tasha off, and that was never a good thing,*" Maddy thought. Rick noticed, got up, and headed for the kitchen while Maddy and Ashley shifted uncomfortably.

"You two sound rather snobistiche. That means snobbish, by the way." Tasha stood up and faced both of them. "What makes you think that a very upscale restaurant wouldn't have a top-notch chef?" She wagged her finger at them. "Do you even have any idea what it costs to eat there? Do you know the history of the chef and what his credentials are?"

"Umm... no, I don't," Maddy admitted.

"Esattamente!" Tasha was not impressed. Her hands were waving everywhere, adding emphasis to what she was saying. "Why would you jump to the conclusion that these knives would somehow be out of his league? Is it because you think I couldn't be working at a nice place? 'Chez Henri' isn't your local 'Pietro' pizza shack, you know!"

"No, Tasha, that's absolutely not what we were thinking!" Ashley rushed to reassure her. "It's more about us thinking that there wasn't such an upscale, Michelin 3-star place in Edmonton. It had nothing to do with you."

"She's right, Tasha, it's not on you, it was us being narrow-minded and jumping to conclusions," Maddy added, trying to mollify her.

"Look here, I know my work isn't as exciting as the art world or even finding expensive paintings in auction units but I'm damn good at my job. Basta! Enough of you being condescending!"

Maddy scooted to the back of her chair, surprised at seeing this side of Tasha. It rarely came out, except when the girls pushed her too far. She was always so outspoken, confident, and also quite level-headed. It was difficult sometimes to remember that she, too, might have insecurities. She felt bad about hurting her friend's feelings.

"We know you are good at whatever you work at, Tasha. You're a smart lady, and anyone would be lucky to have you working for them," Ashley said. "I'm so sorry if we ever gave you the impression we thought otherwise."

"Fine." She sat back down. "I forgive you. I guess I'm feeling a bit sensitive today," Tasha said.

"Why, habibti?" Rick asked after hearing her voice calm down. He came back from the kitchen and sat down beside his wife, putting his arm around her. "You know you're all that," he said.

"Thank you. It's just that I was on Facebook this morning and read a post from a girl I went to school with. She's doing some kind of important research and even has her doctorate. She has achieved so much, it has me wondering about what I have accomplished. Or not accomplished, if you understand me?"

"That's all good and fine, but does she have two beautiful twin girls?" Rick asked. "Does she have a husband who thinks the sun rises and sets with her?"

Tasha laughed and snuggled under her husband's arm. "No, I guess not."

Ashley moved from her chair to the open spot beside Tasha and took her hand.

"We all have times when we get down on ourselves. You're the smartest, funniest, most organized, most compassionate, and loving person I have ever met."

"Hey! What about me?" Maddy pretended to be offended.

"Meh, you're kinda special too."

Chapter 9

TUSDAY

TUESDAY

Ashley was sitting at her desk, closely examining what appeared to be a Ming Dynasty Chinese vase. Using a magnifying glass, she inspected it to ensure it wasn't counterfeit. She examined the glaze, patterns, and maker's marks to assess authenticity. Her concentration was so intense, she almost didn't hear Tasha's call. She was glad she was calling. She felt as though she hadn't been respectful or even aware of what was going on in her friend's life lately, especially after this Sunday's brunch. They had all gotten too caught up in their own lives that it had been easy to simply coast along. Hearing Tasha's perspective was a good reminder for Ashley that all of them were doing their best, and sometimes people need support.

"Hi Tasha!"

"Hello, bella, guess what?"

"What?"

"I've discovered that Edmonton is a very small world," Tasha said.

"Just now?"

"Yeah, right. It never ceases to amaze me," Tasha chuckled. "I spoke with the chef at my restaurant, and not only is he interested in Maddy's knives, he also happens to know the chef who last owned them!"

"You're kidding me! I had heard the previous owner wasn't in the restaurant business anymore," Ashley said.

"That's right. He heard through the grapevine that his knives had shown up in Edmonton."

"Mackenzie said he talks to him once or twice a year, and that he isn't a chef any longer. Mac talked about him like he was a cautionary tale or something."

"Yeah, I've heard some rumors about him. It just goes to show you that, as talented as one may be, it will not help if your behavior ruins your reputation and life."

"That's very true, amica," Tasha said. "We were wondering, would you be able to bring the knives to him? So he can see them up close?"

"Sure, why don't you give me his phone number, and I'll give him a call and set something up."

"Excellent, I will text you his contact information. Thank you. I will let him know that you will be in touch with him soon. He was so excited. Bye!"

Ashley was pleasantly surprised by this call. 'Way to go, Tasha!' she thought to herself. She should have known better than to underestimate that little Italian dynamo friend of hers.

MADDY HAD BEEN THINKING of Tasha's reaction when Ashley had shared with her the news about the chef at her restaurant,

wondering if they could have done more to reassure her. It was not the first time Tasha had come through for them. It had not been fair of them to speak to her that way. She was not only their equal, but most important of all, she was their close friend.

She felt her phone vibrating in her back pocket. Looking at the call display, she didn't recognize the number. She couldn't quite place it or the name accompanying it, Damon Archer. That name did not sound the least familiar. She received so many scam calls that she hesitated to answer. Yet it was a local number, so she took a chance and answered.

"Hello?" she said.

"Hi, is this Maddy Whitman?" the man on the other end asked.

"Yes, it is she."

"My name is Damon Archer. I was given your name by someone who heard you had a set of knives of mine."

"Umm... I have some knives. I don't know if they are yours or not. Who are you exactly?"

"As I said, my name is Damon Archer. I had a storage unit for which I fell behind on the payments. Its contents have been sold at an auction. They're a very valuable set and mean a lot to me."

"I'm aware of their value." 'Here we go again,' Maddy thought. "Unfortunately, I can't just give them back to you."

"Hey, that's cool, I totally get it. You bought the unit fair and square. I'm not arguing that." He sounded calm and logical, not like a crazed lunatic. This was refreshing to Maddy. It was always easier to discuss these matters when both parties were behaving like mature adults.

"I wanted to reach out to you and let you know that they're my knives," he explained. "I'd be willing to pay you back for whatever your final bid was for the unit."

Maddy sat in stunned silence. He wanted to pay $55 to get a knife set worth more than $10,000? Then again, they were his knives, she thought. 'No, I have to stop thinking with my heart, especially after the financial loss I've recently incurred due to Mr. Lumberjack,' she told herself. The knives were not his anymore. He had lost ownership of them when he became delinquent on his payments for the unit rental. That was clearly outlined in the agreement he signed when he got the unit. Of course, if there had been personal items like pictures, letters, or journals, she would have tried to return them.

"I'm sorry, Mr. Archer, that's not possible, however, they will be listed in an auction soon. If you like, I can let you know when and where that will be."

"I can't afford auction prices! Besides, why should I have to buy back my own knives?" His voice was becoming louder. She was concerned that she would soon be the only mature adult in the conversation.

"Truth be told, they are no longer your knives," Maddy informed him. "Triple A took possession of them when you didn't make your payments. You were given several months to make things right and chose not to. When they auctioned them off to me, it was their legal right to do so. I now own the knives, not you."

There was silence on Damon's side. Maddy wasn't quite sure what she was waiting for. She didn't need him to agree with what she had said, but she hoped he would understand her position.

"You better watch your back, damn bitch!" Damon spat out.

"Excuse me?" Maddy was shocked by his reaction. He had gone from 0 to 60 in record time.

"You heard me. Karma's a bitch just like you, and you'll get your own," he said. "You can hide behind technicalities all you want, those knives belong to me."

"I think this conversation is over," Maddy said quietly, pushing the end button. She rose from the couch, body trembling. She had never been good at confrontations, and having someone attack her verbally like that was distinctly off-putting. On the upside, any hesitation she might have felt regarding the knives' ownership was completely gone after his attack. Maddy was fed up with pushy, obnoxious bullies. She was grateful that the men in her life - Rick, Kyle, PopPop, Zane, heck, even Rod - were not like that. Thankfully, not all men she interacted with were jerks.

Chapter 10

WEDNESDAY

The next day, after the lunch rush had ended, Ashley arrived at Chez Henri's, the restaurant where Tasha worked. Having spoken at length with the chef, Mackenzie, they had finally arranged for him to view the knives. Even though they would be going up for auction online, it would not hurt to have some of the potential buyers see them in real life. Tasha was at the front of the restaurant, going over the reservations list for the night. She looked up and grinned at the sight of her friend.

"Well, hello there, Ashley!"

"Hi Tasha, long time no see!"

"How long has it been? Two, three long days?" She laughed, seemingly in a much happier mood than on Sunday.

"When I spoke with Chef Mackenzie, after you and I had our conversation, he said he would be available this afternoon, so here I am," Ashley said.

"I'll let Chef know you're here," Tasha said and turned around, still smiling.

"No need, Tasha, I'm right here. I assume you're Ashley?" Chef Mackenzie Davis said as he came around the corner. He reached out to shake her hand and then motioned for her to join him at one of the tables. "Please, call me Mac."

"Would you like me to send some coffee to your table?" asked Tasha.

"No, thank you, I'm good," Ashley replied. Chef Mac also declined her offer.

"Alright then, I'll leave you two to discuss knives." Off she went to the back of the restaurant. Ashley presumed there was an office or some kind of workspace there.

"I'm very excited to see these knives, I've heard so much about them over the years," he said.

"They are truly exquisite. I didn't know a lot about knives before I saw these. What I'm learning is quite fascinating." Ashley smiled as she pulled the knife roll out of the carryall bag she had brought along. Laying it out on the table, she ceremoniously unrolled it and waited for the chef to inspect its contents.

"Oh my, they are perfection, aren't they?" he said as he took one of the knives in his hands, weighing the feel of them. "Such lovely balance." He then looked at the edge and heel of the blade of one of the carving knives, turning it around and gently running a finger over the handle.

"This one here is a fowl carving knife. It was specifically used to carve quail," Ashley explained, as though she had always known knives. "It's a Masashi Kuroshu Honesuki knife."

"A woman after my own heart!" he said with a voice like tanned leather. "Did Tasha tell you that quail is a specialty of mine?"

"No, she didn't."

"Well, it is, and you are in luck! I've started some for tonight. Would you like to come back into the kitchen to see? Maybe I could even try the knife out?"

"I'm afraid I can't allow that, it's against policy. As you can see, the knives are in excellent condition, and we can't risk anything happening to them."

"Oh, I understand, no need to apologize. You know, I don't even need to try them. I'm willing to make you an offer right now," he said.

"I wish I could accept your offer, unfortunately, I can't." Ashley was quite pleased to see how interested he was. "As you are aware, it will be going up for auction soon. You'll have to compete with the other chefs if you want to end up with these! Don't worry, I'll give you the details for the auction, of course."

"Can't blame a guy for trying." He winked at her and rolled up the knives. He then invited Ashley to follow him to the back of the restaurant, where the kitchen was. "I have, if I do say so myself, perfected the quail dish first made popular by Joel Robuchon, also known as 'La Caille.'"

"'The Quail'? Ashley laughed.

"Vous parlez français! Yes, simplicity at its finest, even in the dish's name. Don't let that fool you, though. This dish involves using a free-range quail. It is stuffed with foie gras, glazed with some soy and a touch of honey, and then served with truffle mashed potato. Exquisite!" Chef Mackenzie emphasized his description by bringing together two fingers and his thumb and kissing them, the ultimate 'Chef's Kiss'.

He proceeded to show Ashley how to prepare 'La Caille', step by step.

"First, you remove the legs. I will cook these separately. Then, you trim off the wings, like this." Off came the wings, one by one. "Then you find the breast and make space to stuff the foie gras in." He noticed Ashley's look of uncertainty. "Don't worry, I make sure to only buy foie gras that is from range-free, humanely raised ducks and geese, right here in Alberta."

"That's a relief." Ashley smiled. She didn't like the idea of birds being force-fed to fatten their livers.

After some time, Ashley made her apologies. She had to get back to work, and this process of preparing quail was taking much longer than she had anticipated.

"Thank you so much, Chef MacKenzie, as much as I would love to stay and learn how to prepare this amazing dish, I must get back to my office."

"Please, call me Mac or Chef. Chef Mackenzie makes me sound so pompous." He smiled at her with the most amazing eyes that Ashley had seen in a long time. They seemed to be looking deep into her soul. Leaving Chef Mac was going to be difficult, but she had too much work waiting for her.

"Alright, I shall," she replied with a smile. "I can't wait to come back one evening and have a chance to try the full experience of dining at Chez Henri's, and, of course, have a taste of 'La Caille.'"

"Make sure you let whoever serves you know that I want to be notified you are here," he said. "I will make sure to prepare something extra special."

"You know how to tempt a girl, don't you?" Ashley said teasingly as they walked up to the front, where Tasha was standing once again.

"It was a pleasure to meet you, Ashley," he said, taking both of her hands in his as he spoke. "I look forward to seeing you again."

Tasha waited until he had walked out of earshot before turning to her friend.

"Were you flirting?" she asked.

"Maybe a little," Ashley replied. "He is quite handsome and appears to be very talented with his hands."

Tasha gave her a knowing smile.

They stood and chatted for a bit until Ashley said goodbye and headed for her car. She was halfway there when she realized she had left her carryall bag with the knives in the restaurant. She turned around swiftly, cursing her forgetfulness. Those knives were worth too much to leave lying around. As she returned to the restaurant, Chef Mac was walking toward her, bag in hand.

"I don't think you want to forget this," he said with a smile. "I might be tempted to claim that possession is nine-tenths of the law or something similar, but I wouldn't want you to think badly of me." He gave her his warmest smile.

She thanked him, took her bag out of his hands, and retraced her steps back toward her car after promising him, once again, that she would return for dinner soon.

BACK IN HER CAR, PATIENCE not being her strong suit, Ashley excitedly placed a call to Maddy.

"I think we have a serious bidder for your knives!" she blurted out, not bothering with pleasantries. "Let me rephrase that,"

Ashley thought it best to give credit where credit was due. "Tasha came through for us! Her Chef Mackenzie from Chez Henri's is more than a little interested. He wants them badly! He was ready to take them off my hands immediately!"

"That's exciting news! Why don't you meet me at Blendz, and you can tell me all about it?"

"I have a meeting to go to soon. I could meet you right after." They arranged to meet at the coffee shop across the street from Maddy's apartment.

To say that Maddy was happy about Chef Mackenzie's interest would have been an understatement. She vowed never to minimize what Tasha had to say again. If there could be more than one chef interested in her knives, and they counterbid each other, it would more than make up for the insurance deductible, much, much more. She took advantage of the time she had before meeting with Ashley to submit the insurance claim for the break-in. Her agent had assured her that everything would be covered. She also told her that if she could send pictures of the broken items that were collectibles, the ones she hadn't filed photographs of before the break-in, they would offer her more than replacement value. She explained to Maddy that since they were collectibles, they would pay her the minimum value of a non-perfect item. This was wonderful news to her. She was going to make some money after all. Other than the headache of cleaning up the mess, there would only be a minor loss on a couple of items. Thankfully, not one big enough to do any damage to her long-range plans for her dream store. Things were looking up for her. What a wonderful feeling that was.

ON THE WAY TO MEET Maddy, Ashley thought back on what she had learned at the restaurant. There certainly were people interested in knives of this quality in Edmonton, and she most definitely wanted to try out the Chef's creations. Perhaps, she could even get to know him better, too.

It had been easy to spot Maddy as soon as she entered the coffee shop. She found her sitting in her favorite spot, a booth near the front window, looking out onto the sidewalk. From there, she had a view of the traffic on Jasper Avenue and all the comings and goings. Maddy did not like to miss anything.

"Did you order my tea already?" she asked.

"Of course I did, it will be up with my coffee." Maddy had ordered her a ginger lemon caffeine-free tea with a spoonful of organic honey.

"Thanks, you know me so well."

"Yup, you know you're good friends when you not only know what the other person drinks but also at what time of the day they switch to herbal tea," Maddy said.

"Well, we can't all drink coffee after three and still sleep like a baby."

"Maggie W!" the barista yelled. "I think this might be for me."

"Hey, it's closer than last time, eh, "Madgie with A Man?" Both laughed at the memory of so many misnomers.

Maddy rose and went to pick up their drinks. She grabbed a couple of napkins and brought everything back to the booth.

"So, Tasha's chef was interested, was he?"

"He most definitely was," Ashley said. "He wanted to make me an offer on the spot."

"He did?" Maddy's eyes widened in excitement. "What did you say?"

"I told him what I would tell anyone, that they need to wait for the auction, even if he was very handsome. I mean, we could accept an offer for a guaranteed amount, but the whole point of the auction is to make top dollar. And we need to do that so you can get into your store sooner rather than later."

"Speaking of which, what do you think about 'Maddy's Mayhem' for a store name?"

"No." Ashley's answer was fast and decisive. "Why not?"

"It doesn't say what business you're in, and it sounds too chaotic. Like you don't know what you're doing."

"Okay, I guess it's back to the drawing board," Maddy said, not sounding too defeated.

"You're getting there. It beats your last suggestion of 'Slightly Used, Totally Confused'"

"I'll keep trying then," Maddy said, smiling as she sipped her coffee. "Wait a minute! Did you say he was very handsome?"

"That I did."

"Spill it!"

"I'm pretty sure he was flirting with me. I certainly was flirting back. I'll be going back for dinner one evening. I think that I'll go by myself, just in case he is interested..."

"Well, who do we have here?" a voice rang out. Turning around, Maddy saw the woman approaching, a large, toothy grin on her face.

"Oh dear," Maddy whispered to Ashley.

"Hi, Paris." She met Paris here on occasion to show her something that could be of interest to one of her clients, but she didn't think it was a regular haunt for the woman.

Paris sat down beside Maddy, forcing her to move over to make room.

"Hello, how have you been?" Paris said, ignoring Maddy and focusing her attention on Ashley. Paris thought of Ashley as her peer, making Maddy quite aware that she didn't meet their level of qualifications or intelligence.

"I'm doing well, thank you. Maddy and I were just discussing an upcoming international online auction. She has a collection that we are putting in it," Ashley said.

"Really?" Paris turned to look at Maddy, the surprise evident on her face.

"Yes, a set of high-end knives. If you know of anyone who may be into collecting chefs' knives or who might be chefs themselves, let them know about the auction," Ashley said, never missing an opportunity to spread the word. "Of course, there will be a finder's fee if you recommend someone who posts the highest bid," she added, much to Paris' surprise and pleasure.

"Oh, I shall most definitely do that."

There was a lull in the conversation, and Paris stood up to order a drink. Maddy looked at Ashley over the table and rolled her eyes. Ashley just smiled and sipped her tea.

Walking back to the table, Paris peered at Ashley's bag, which was on the floor beside her.

"Well, look at that, we have the same carryall bag!" Paris lifted the bag she was carrying to show Ashley.

"Yes, it looks like we do."

"It's such a great bag with a place for everything! Where did you get yours?" Paris asked. "It can't be from around here, there just aren't many great places to get good designer items in the city."

"Oh, I don't remember," Ashley said. "You're probably correct, though. I must have picked it up somewhere during one of my business trips."

Maddy knew that while she always looked stylish and put together, Ashley wasn't one to pay much attention to things like brand names.

"Oh hey, did you hear from a guy called Chad? I recommended you to him the other day," Maddy said.

Ashley gave Maddy a questioning look, which the latter ignored.

"Yes, I did, I saw his place yesterday. I certainly have my work cut out for me. The man simply has no taste to speak of." Paris wrinkled her nose as though she had smelled something foul.

'Of course, why would she thank me for the referral?' Maddy thought.

"Thanks for the coffee, Ashley," Maddy said. "I do have to get going."

"Thank you. I believe you were the one who bought today," Ashley smiled while lifting her mug of tea in a mock salute.

"Guess next one will be your treat then. I gotta go, see you soon!" Maddy left the table, not only to escape spending more time with Paris than necessary, but also because she had a pile of work waiting back at her apartment. She was almost out of earshot when she heard Paris tell Ashley that they really should get together and do lunch one of these days. It was obvious to Maddy that this horrible woman was trying to befriend Ashley.

"How is business going?" Paris asked Ashley.

"Oh, you know, busy as usual."

Paris shifted in her seat. "Yes, this business..."

They sat there for a moment before Paris tried again.

"I've been very busy. Lots of people out there who need someone to guide them in the right direction, interior design-wise, you know? I shudder to think of what their homes would look like without me to help them find just the right piece, I'm sure you understand."

"To be honest, most of my clients are high-end collectors; they are looking for specific pieces more than help with decorating," Ashley replied. She knew she was bordering on rudeness, but she didn't like the way Paris acted around Maddy, as if she barely existed. She had practically shoved her aside when she had imposed herself at their table. No one treated her best friend this way and could expect her to sit around and not take notice. Ashley had met a lot of women like her. She was under no illusion that if she bought and sold auction locker items, Paris wouldn't give her the time of day.

"Oh, yes, of course. I'm aware of the quality and class of your clientele," Paris gushed.

"Listen, Paris, I'm sorry, I don't mean to be rude, but I have to make an important phone call right away. I'm sure you understand how it is in our business." Ashley put her hand over her cell phone, which was sitting between them on the table.

"I absolutely understand. A big part of our profession is taking meetings and chatting up potential clients." Paris smiled as she sat back in her seat. Ashley continued to stare at her, her hand not moving. It took Paris about three seconds to realize she was being asked to leave.

"Well, yes, then, I best get going. Money doesn't make itself, you know," Paris said as she scooted out of the booth. Ashley made her call, and it was ringing through as Paris reached down and grabbed her bag, which was on the floor next to Ashley's bag. She waved at Ashley as she left the coffee shop. There was a look of self-satisfaction on Paris's face as she walked away, which made Ashley a tad uneasy.

Checking in with the receptionist at her office, Ashley wanted to verify if a package she had been expecting had finally arrived. Not exactly an important call requiring privacy, still, she made the call, not wanting anyone to ever call her a liar. After her call, she finished her last sip of tea and grabbed her bag to leave. The bag felt light, much lighter than it should have.

"Shit!" For a fleeting moment, she wondered if maybe Paris had taken the knives out of her bag. She quickly discarded that idea as Paris wouldn't be able to do anything with them without Ashley knowing she had taken them. Opening up the bag, all she saw were some papers, a makeup bag covered with overlapping L's and V's, and a matching wallet in Paris's bag.

Now what was she going to do? Paris was long gone, and she was stuck with her bag. More importantly, the knives were out of her sight, and all her personal items were in that woman's hands. Luckily, Ashley had a pair of keys hidden in her vehicle. She knew it wasn't the smartest thing to do, however, it had saved her behind more than once. Luckily, her cell had been on the table, and her house keys were in her suit pocket. She should have brought along a purse, too, instead of putting everything in her carryall. The mix-up might not have happened if she had simply carried a large purse.

'You won't believe what happened!' Ashley texted Maddy.

'Oh no, what?'

'Paris left with my bag.'

"SHE STOLE IT?'

'No, I don't think so. She must have mixed her bag up with mine. They are identical after all.'

'Uh-huh. How can I help?'

'Can you send me her phone number? Hopefully she can get back here quickly.'

A second later, Maddy texted the requested contact information. Ashley immediately dialed the number but it went directly to voicemail.

"Hello, Paris? This is Ashley. We seem to have had a mix-up with our bags. Could you please call me back as soon as possible? Thank you." Ashley flopped back down in the booth. It didn't look like trying to catch her before she got too far was going to work. She contemplated whether she should wait or just head back to the office. After five minutes had gone by and Paris had not yet returned her call, she decided to leave. Knowing Paris, that woman would be more than happy to meet her there. She would probably ask for a tour and gush over Ashley's colleagues. Not wanting to wait for Paris to check her messages, she fired off a text asking her if she was in the vicinity and if she could meet Ashley at her office. She then provided the address. As she drove to her office, she couldn't help but wonder if that smug look on Paris's face when she left had anything to do with the carryall switch. Could she be that sneaky? Ashley liked to give people the benefit of the doubt, yet she had a feeling from what she had heard from Maddy that this should not apply to Paris.

Chapter 11

A shley was having difficulty concentrating on her work.
She drummed her fingers on her desk and kept looking at her smartwatch every ten minutes or so. Patience was not one of her greatest virtues, and she had none for people who ignored her messages, especially important ones. If she was too busy to return a call, then she would text a reply when she had a moment or ask her assistant to do so. It was becoming obvious that Paris did not respect other people's time. It took Paris several hours before she called her back. As soon as she answered, Paris immediately started talking.

"I'm so sorry, Ashley, I don't know what happened. I must have picked up the wrong bag when I left. They are identical after all. I guess that's one of the dangers of us having the same excellent fashion taste." She laughed. It sounded artificial and exaggerated to Ashley's ear.

No apologies were given for the delayed response. Maddy was right, this woman was the epitome of rudeness.

"It's no problem at all, these things happen,' Ashley replied. "Unfortunately, I need the contents of my carryall as soon as possible. Will you, by any chance, be downtown again today?" Now that she thought about it, Ashley had no idea where Paris lived or worked.

"Regretfully, not today. I have several meetings with huge clients. But I will be going downtown tomorrow. There's this gorgeous Lalique crystal vase that I must pick up for a client. A rare piece in this end of the world, as I'm sure you are well aware. Anyway, I digress, why don't we meet for lunch before my meeting – on me – as an apology for the inconvenience?"

"Thank you for the kind offer, but I'm busy over the next few days and won't be able to take the time off to have lunch outside the office. Would you be able to courier it over? That might be even cheaper than lunch." Ashley didn't feel like spending any more time than necessary with Paris. She was not the type of person she wanted to befriend. After witnessing Paris's disrespect and rudeness toward Maddy firsthand, Ashley was not interested in spending unnecessary time with that woman. She wanted her carryall back and nothing more.

"Oh no, I couldn't entrust anybody else with that bag. I'll bring it by your office myself tomorrow," Paris said.

"That would be perfect, thank you, Paris."

"Oh no, please, don't mention it. It's the least I can do for you. Who knows? Maybe you'll find yourself in need of a break when I get there. You know what they say, all work and no play makes Ashley a dull girl!"

"It also makes for a very fulfilled Ashley," Ashley lobbed back. 'Dull, my sweet patootie,' she thought. "If I'm not available when you come by, please just leave it with the receptionist, it'll be safe with her."

There was a pregnant pause at the other end of the call. Ashley could almost feel Paris glaring at her phone. It would appear that this woman might not give up easily.

"Fine, I'll do that," disappointment and anger could be felt as she bit out the words.

When she hung up, Ashley said a silent prayer, hoping she wouldn't regret making an enemy of her. With that type, you never knew how they would take rejection.

Alyssa popped her head through the doorway. "There's a French guy with a weird accent on line two. He's talking nonsense and mentioned those knives we're auctioning off for Ms. Whitman. What do you want me to do?"

"Did he sound interested in them, or was he simply fishing for information?"

"He sounded pretty serious about them. He said he was very close to the person who had made them."

"That was decades ago. I can't imagine anyone would still be alive from back then." Ashley was doubtful about this man, however, her curiosity got the better of her. "Alright, put him through."

"Bonjour madame, I am Chef François. These knives that are in your possession are very, very special to me."

"Hello Monsieur, that's wonderful news. I am sure you will be happy to know that the set of knives is going up for auction very soon.

"Wonderful, yes. I was hoping perhaps that when the auction is about to be over, you could place a bid of five more dollars in my name."

"That would go against all professional auction rules. I'm sorry, that's simply not possible."

"You do not understand. I am the reincarnation of Chef Akira Wataru. These knives were made for him, I mean made for me."

"I'm sorry, you're what?" Alyssa had not been exaggerating when she said that man was talking nonsense. Ashley could not believe what she was hearing.

"It is not a 'what', it's a 'who' ", Chef François continued, insisting that he was Chef Wataru.

"I understand that the knives must go to auction, and I am willing to pay whatever it costs to get them back. It is only a small favor that I am asking for, as insurance, vous comprenez?"

"Oh, I understand quite well." Ashley was blown away by this man's nerve. "This conversation is going nowhere, sir."

"S'il vous plaît, Madame, I AM Chef Akira Wataru, only in another, younger, and healthier body. They are meant to be mine! Especially the quail knife."

"You'll have to try your luck at the online auction, Chef François, au revoir!" Ashley had had enough of a conversation that was going nowhere. She hung up and turned her chair around to look out the window at the traffic far below.

Could this week get any weirder and more frustrating? Ashley wondered. Thankfully, this day was over. She couldn't wait to get home, soak in a hot bubble bath, and forget about the world.

THURSDAY

"ASHLEY, THERE'S A MAN here to see you." Alyssa had poked her head into Ashley's office to let her know. The next morning had arrived much too soon for Ashley's liking. Now, an unexpected visitor was interrupting her after she had just walked into her office a few minutes prior and barely had had the time to turn her computer on. "He said his name is Damon Archer," Alyssa added.

Ashley groaned, throwing back her head and closing her eyes. Maddy had told her about her encounter with the former owner of the storage unit. 'Just what I need,' she thought. 'One more kook to continue on this week's parade of frustrating people.' She was not looking forward to what would, more than likely, turn out to be a showdown with him.

"Ok, I'll be there in a second," Ashley answered. Reaching down into a desk drawer, she pulled out her office emergency makeup bag. She had a feeling this next encounter would be like heading into war, and she needed to feel strong and on top of her game. Fresh lipstick reapplied, she headed out to the reception area. What she saw was a reedy, thin-looking man nervously pacing. He appeared to be in his late 40s, early 50s, with a full head of salt and pepper hair. He was far from being a Chef Mackenzie.

"Mr. Archer?"

"Yes, but please, call me Damon," he said.

"Nice to meet you, I'm Ashley Mueller." She smiled, hoping to keep things civil and avoid a confrontation.

"Please, won't you follow me?" She turned around and led him into her office. Taking a seat behind her desk, in what was considered a position of power in the business world, she looked at him expectantly as he, in turn, sat down on the armchair facing her.

"And how may I be of help to you?" Shifting uncomfortably in the chair, he looked around her office and at the panoramic view from her windows.

"Nice digs you have here," he commented. "Kitchens don't tend to be so fancy or have great views."

She smiled and waited for him to continue.

"So, ummm... I recently found out that you have in your possession a set of knives I had stored in a unit in town."

"That's correct."

"Yeah, and I was wanting to come and make you an offer for them," he said.

"An offer? I can't take any offers. My apologies for your having come all the way downtown, but you see, they will be in an auction soon. I can provide you with the information for it so you can participate in the bidding. You can then place your bid with all the others." Ashley gave him her most disarming smile.

"Oh no, there is no need for that. I'm willing to purchase them now," he said. "I could make payments every month and have them paid off in no time."

"I'm afraid that is not within my capacity as my client's agent," she said. "They have hired us to auction them off. We can't just sell them. There are other chefs interested in bidding on them. Just yesterday, a French chef told me he was the original owner."

"What? That's not true, I AM their owner! That Whitman woman bought my storage unit, and it had MY knives and other family heirlooms in it!" He was quickly getting worked up. "And that French chef, was his name 'François' by any chance?"

"I can't give you the names of other potential bidders," Ashley replied. She wished she had asked Alyssa to keep an eye on their meeting and be prepared to call security if necessary.

"Listen here, Chef François is nutso. He thinks he's the reincarnation of every damn chef who died and collects their knives. Chef Akira Wataru is just the latest one. I am the rightful owner of those knives, not that walking lunatic in a chef's toque!"

"The rightful, legal owner is Maddy Whitman, not you. She has proof of purchase from the auctioneer and the storage facility. She has instructed us to auction them off. That's what we are obligated to do. If you would like information on the auction, I can..."

"NO!" The chef stood up, placing his hands on her desk and leaning forward. "Those are my knives, I'm doing you a favor by making you an offer!" he yelled at her. "You expect me to compete with others to pay for my own knives? Lady, you're certifiably crazy."

At that moment, Alyssa walked up to her office, put her hands on opposite sides of the door frame, and leaned in.

"Hey, Ashley, the men are waiting for you in the boardroom. Would you like me to tell them you're tied up?"

"No, thank you, Alyssa. I think we are finished here," she said while gathering a pen and paper from her desk. "I'll see you out, Mr. Archer." She motioned toward her office door.

"I'll do that, Ashley, you go to your meeting. The men have been waiting for a few minutes already. They look like they're getting impatient." Alyssa made eye contact with her. Ashley could not help but notice her use of the word 'men' instead of 'partners' as was customary, not once but twice. They both knew she did not have a meeting. In addition, very few of the people who worked in the office were men, certainly not enough to fill a meeting room.

They left her office. Damon Archer mumbled something under his breath that sounded like a threat; even so, it was not clear enough to call security. Ashley nodded to Alyssa, turned right, and walked down the hall.

"Hello gentlemen," she said in a loud voice as she entered the empty boardroom. "My apologies for making you wait," she added, closing the door behind her.

A few minutes later, Alyssa opened the door and walked in. "Coast's clear," she declared.

"Thank you so much, Alyssa. That was quick thinking on your part! You're amazing," Ashley said. "I was just sitting there thinking I should have asked you to interrupt us with some kind of excuse after five or ten minutes, and poof, there you were."

"Once I heard him start to yell, I figured things risked escalating pretty fast."

"I'm so grateful, but you didn't have to put yourself in the line of fire. I could have walked him out," Ashley said.

"I thought that if it was someone whom he hadn't yelled at yet, it might calm things down."

"Smart! Next time, call security first, just in case the person is truly dangerous."

Alyssa's eyes twinkled as she grinned widely. "I did. I just called them back to let them know it had been a false alarm right after he left."

"Well then, I guess you have things well under control," Ashley laughed. "I owe you lunch."

"Deal! I like Campio's pizza, in case you were wondering." They both laughed.

"Any time you like, just give me a day or two's notice."

"Ding! Ding!" The bell at the reception desk rang insistently. The two women exchanged worried glances, thinking Archer had returned for more.

"Let me go check," Alyssa said.

"No, I will. If he's back, I'll deal with him."

"But he'll know you're not in a meeting!"

"Too bad, the time for niceties is over," Ashley said, steel in her voice.

They walked back down the hall together toward the reception area. As they turned the corner, Ashley felt conflicting emotions. It wasn't Damon Archer standing there, it was Paris.

She had told Alyssa that if a Paris Andrews showed up, to tell her Ashley was busy, but now they were face to face.

"Paris!"

Alyssa looked at her, wide-eyed. Ashley shook her head, letting her know that it was alright.

"Hi Ashley, so glad you're available." Ashley noticed a tone in Paris' voice, a sarcastic sounding one, like she knew Ashley didn't want to see her. 'Oh well, time to bite the bullet and be civil.' Ashley thought.

"Hello, Paris. Thank you for coming all the way here. Won't you come into my office?"

As they walked through her office door, Paris gasped.

"Oh my god, this is beautiful, look at that view! You've been holding out on me, you didn't tell me you had a corner office!" Paris said, over-enthused.

"It's not something that comes up in conversation much," Ashley replied, an ungracious thought occurring to her that if the roles were reversed, Paris would find a way to slip it into any exchange.

"Here's your bag," she reached into her bottom drawer to retrieve it and then passed it to Paris.

"Excellent, and again I apologize for my carelessness."

"Mistakes happen." Ashley remained standing behind her desk. "Thanks again for coming here to drop it off."

"It's the least I could do," Paris waved her off. "By the way, I opened up the bag – that's how I found out it wasn't mine – and I noticed you had a knife roll in it. Is that the one you were talking about? I didn't want to open it up and pry."

'Of course you didn't,' Ashley thought. 'But I bet you couldn't help yourself.'

"Yes, those are Maddy's knives."

"Well, as I promised, if I hear of anyone who would be interested, I'll pass the info along," Paris said.

"I appreciate that. It's always good to spread out information as far and wide as possible. That's why we're doing an international auction. These auction houses usually have the connections to advertise."

"Yes, of course, an extremely smart business move on your part," Paris cooed, almost drooling. "I guess that's why you ended up with the corner office, right?"

"Something like that," Ashley's smile was tight.

"May I see the knives? I would like to take pictures and send them to some of my clients."

"I'm afraid not, it wouldn't be right to give anyone an unfair advantage now, would it, Paris? Her smile became tighter. "I'll text you the link, and you can forward it to your clients."

"Oh, darn it, but I understand." Paris gave her a childish pout. "Are you sure you don't have time for a lunch date today, or even a coffee?"

"Sorry, Paris, I'm truly swamped today. I'll be eating at my desk." That certainly wasn't a lie. She had packed a salad for work this morning. It was now waiting for her in the office refrigerator.

"I don't mind keeping you company. I'll call a restaurant delivery service."

"Your thoughtfulness is appreciated, but again, I'm very, very busy. It's not possible today." Ashley thought that woman was like a dog with a bone. At some point, she would have to take 'no' for an answer.

"Maybe another time then," Paris turned around to leave. "Don't get up on my account, I'll see myself out." Paris apparently had received this hint loud and clear.

Ashley nodded, not even bothering to feign getting up to walk her to the door. Rudeness was something she disliked, but sometimes, the situation called for it.

Chapter 12

FRIDAY

"Oh my God, this hamburger is to die for!" drooled Sophia. "Mom never lets us eat hamburgers and fries."

"Don't exaggerate, Soph. Mom lets us eat burgers and fries.

She doesn't let you eat TWO burgers with double servings of fries," Chloe corrected her twin.

Sophia rolled her eyes at her sister. "Either way, this hamburger is the best."

"I thought you might enjoy a Woodshed Burger meal after Karate," Maddy told them.

"You thought YOU would enjoy a Woodshed Burger, admit it," laughed Ashley.

Maddy and Ashley had picked up their goddaughters from their Karate class. Mama Leila was busy baking for a fundraiser, so they had been called to the rescue this evening. Maddy wasn't usually busy on Fridays, so the last-minute request from Rick's mother hadn't been a problem. Surprisingly, though, Ashley had also been free.

"Karate always makes me hungry," Sophia remarked.

"I honestly don't get why Baba wants us to take martial arts lessons," Chloe said. "It's not like we can't defend ourselves."

"Yeah," added Sophia. "A swift kick in the cajones, and down the guy goes."

Maddy and Ashley roared with laughter.

"Sophia, what if it's a woman who attacks you?" asked Ashley.

"Or, what if it's TWO guys?" added Maddy. "Karate will help you deal with multiple people at a time. Like in Karate Kid."

"Karate Kid?" asked Chloe.

"The movies that came out before Cobra Kai," replied Sophia.

"Oh. Well, I still think we can defend ourselves without taking a Karate lesson." Chloe insisted. "Although the guys in our Dojo are kind of cute."

"Speaking of cute guys... Auntie Ash, how come you don't have a date tonight? You tend to be busy on Friday nights," asked Sophia.,

"Yeah, Auntie Ash, what gives?" joined Maddy, pleased that her goddaughter had asked the question that had been on her mind.

"How rude!" Chloe interjected. "You don't ask people why they don't have dates!"

"How correct you are, Chloe," Ashley replied. "I knew there was a reason you were my favorite of the two of you."

"Talk about being rude, I'm offended! " Sophia crossed her arms and feigned to be upset.

"There are no secrets between BFF's and goddaughters.

Spill it, girlfriend." Maddy smirked.

"Fine! I ended things with the gentleman I was seeing," Ashley replied. "Satisfied?"

"No more Barry, or Larry then? I can't keep track of their names," said Maddy.

"Me neither," added Sophia.

"It was Garry. What's so hard about that name to remember?" Chloe came to the rescue.

"Right again, Miss Chloe. I know which one of you to include in my will." She gave Sophia a side-eye look.

"What about that chef ? Mackenzie, was it?" Maddy asked.

"Mom's boss?" Chloe looked at Ashley with a raised brow. "Now he's one hottie!" Sophia observed.

"When did you meet him? Mom only started working there last week?"

"Ever heard of a thing called the Internet, Chloe dear?" Sophia threw back.

"You looked him up online? My sister, the online stalker."

"Enough, you two. Chloe, your sister is not a stalker," Maddy came to Sophia's defense. "I looked him up too, after Ash said they had flirted."

"Maddy! You don't need to tell them everything!" Ashley then turned to the girls, "We hit it off, girls, that's all."

"That's great!" Chloe said.

"When are you going out on a date with the delicious Chef Mackenzie?"

"Sophia!" Both Ashley and Chloe reacted in mock shock.

"Well, when are you?" asked Maddy.

"I don't know. I did tell him that I wanted to try his stuffed quail, and he said to make sure to let him know when I was coming to the restaurant so he could treat me special."

"Ooooh!" both girls sighed, their romantic hearts warming.

"Yeah, oooh... stuffed quail..." Maddy said, looking as taken as the twins, but for a different reason.

"Why don't you go tomorrow evening? Mom doesn't have a shift," Sophia suggested. This way, she won't be snooping, and you can have privacy," she added and winked at Ashley.

"Hmm... Good idea. I just might reinstate you in my will after all."

WHILE THE TWINS WERE washing up, Ashley turned to Maddy and asked her if she had heard anything from PopPop about talking to Bob.

"Yeah, I sure did. We chatted on the phone last night, apparently, he and Shirley talked about it." Maddy told her.

"And?"

"Well, he told me that Shirley was a bit evasive. She seemed more reluctant to talk to Bob than PopPop expected. I think he thought she would break up with Bob and they would continue as a regular couple. It sounds like she may not be as ready to choose which one she's willing to settle with, as PopPop thought she might be. After having dated him for a bit, he was certain that he would be the obvious choice," Maddy explained.

"Oh my," Ashley widened her eyes and leaned forward, eager to engage in the drama. "What do you think she'll do?"

"PopPop pushed the issue and said he would not continue to go behind another man's back."

"Good for him!"

"That's what I told him, too. So, she called Bob and they're supposed to get together in a few days."

"I'm so glad to hear she is going to deal with this, no matter which man she decides on," Ashley said, sitting back.

"I'm a bit uneasy about it, to tell you the truth," Maddy said. "They're going together to talk to Bob. The two of them."

"Oh my!" Ashley leaned forward again. "To be a fly on the wall for that!"

"Right? I wonder how that will play out!"

"You wonder how what will play out?" Chloe asked as she and her sister slid into their seats.

"Nothing for you to worry about," Maddy said, smiling at the girls. In turn, the twins looked at each other and rolled their eyes.

"Fine, we won't pry into your 'adult' conversation," Sophia said while doing air quotes.

Chapter 13

SATURDAY

"This is a lovely little park, Randy." Shirley looked around, admiring their surroundings. "I didn't even know a place like this existed in Edmonton!"

"My granddaughter brought me here; that's how I know about it." PopPop was happy that Shirley liked his choice for a date. "We first went for an ice cream at the Kind Ice Cream Store like you and I just did, then she suggested we walk over to Paul Kane Park and sit by the pond to watch the little family of ducks that were here. Looks like they've gone south already."

"That sounds like a perfect outing with Maddy. I wish that I had a grandchild to dote on. Alas," she sighed, "it wasn't meant to be."

"Perhaps one day you can be a step-grandmother. You know, I'm not her biological grandfather. I don't have any blood grandchildren." He held her hand as they walked. "I'm lucky that she cares about me like that. I grew so attached to her when she was little."

"It must have been so hard not to see her for all those years. Imagine thinking you were dead!"

"Yeah, my son is something else." PopPop looked away, his thoughts taking him beyond the pond.

"He's still alive?"

"Yes, but I want nothing to do with him. He's cruel and a drunk. I don't know where I went wrong raising him."

"Parents can only give their children the tools. What they do with them is not in your control. It's not your fault." She gave him a gentle kiss on the cheek.

"I feel for Maddy." Shirley's heart went out to her. "Such a nice young woman. Having had to deal with a terrible stepfather, a mom dying of cancer, and then losing you."

"She turned out okay, though, mostly because of her friends." PopPop felt somewhat guilty for not having tried harder to reach out to his granddaughter. "If only that dark cloud of bad luck would stop following her!"

"Did she put the crystals I gave her in her house and locker? She needs good chakra around her."

"She did."

"Good! Has she heard from the insurance company yet?"

"Yes, she's going to end up with some money in her pocket after all. It's not going to be a loss. She might have made more if she had sold them, but in her business, you never know. At least she made the minimum amount."

"So, the crystals worked!"

"They sure did, sweetheart." He didn't have the heart to tell her that Maddy had already heard back from the insurance company before placing the crystals. PopPop preferred to let her think that she had done something positive for his Maddy.

They walked a little longer, finishing their ice cream cones. He was enjoying her company. It had been a long time since he had had female companionship.

"Tell me about Hawaii. What happened there with your ex? If you don't mind my asking," PopPop said.

"It's quite the sad story. Let's sit on this bench, I'll tell you all about it." Shirley pointed to a concrete bench with wooden slats on it, facing the lake.

She prefaced her story by telling him that there was a lot more involved with what had happened in Hawaii.

"I don't want my nephew to worry or to think I'm a doddering old woman," she explained. "I hope you won't think any less of me either."

"Of course not, my sweet, you can tell me anything and I will still think the sun rises and sets by your smile." He picked up her hand and kissed the back of it.

Shirley began by telling him that she had met Stanley on an online dating site for seniors. He was the perfect gentleman. After three months of dating, he suggested they go to Hawaii and elope. Stan made it all sound so romantic. He bought her a beautiful diamond ring, flowers, and everything for their ceremony by the sea. It was the two of them, the justice of the peace, and two hotel staff members acting as witnesses. They got married as the sun was setting.

"It was perfect," Shirley said. "Until it was not."

One day, he claimed that someone had stolen his credit cards. Another day, the bank had frozen his accounts in Canada. Then, he ran out of all the cash he had on him.

"I see where this is going," remarked PopPop.

"That's exactly where it went, downhill." Shirley continued her story. At first, she gave him the benefit of the doubt because he had spoiled her rotten leading up to the wedding. They rented an oceanfront condo, which she paid for. She had Rod ship most of her Betty Boop collectibles so she could decorate their place. He was very attentive to her. Then, he started borrowing money for gambling. When she refused to give him anymore, her Betty Boops started disappearing. Small ones at first, then more valuable ones.

"Did you confront him?" PopPop asked.

"I did. He denied it. So, I kicked him out of the apartment. I wasn't going to take anymore crap from him."

"Good for you!"

"Well, you would think," she replied. "Because the apartment was a rental, I couldn't change the locks. He snuck in one day when I was out and took whatever cash was in our safe and the TV I had bought him as a wedding present." She sighed and started playing with the bangle on her wrist. "He also took all my Betty Boop collection pieces that were there. Those were worth hundreds of thousands of dollars! They took me years to find and be able to purchase. Thankfully, the place was too small for all of my Betties. I had some in storage. Those are the ones you saw in the back office at Triple A's."

"The nerve of him! That's so incredibly cowardly!" PopPop exclaimed.

"That's not all. The next day, he served me with divorce papers!"

She wanted him out of her life without having a dragged-out divorce. She agreed to everything he was asking for, including a large chunk of money, as long as there would be no alimony. He tried to argue that he deserved alimony. She told him that he would have to take her to court if he wanted more. He knew that the chances of a judge taking his side were slim, so he agreed.

"And that was the end of that. I had fallen out of love with Stan as fast as I had fallen for him," she said.

"When things go sideways and you get angry at someone you love," PopPop said. "The heartache is quickly over."

"With a son like yours, you have experience in that department, I would guess," Shirley remarked. "Anyway, enough of that! Let's talk about your ganja shop."

"Better not let Maddy hear you call it that." He laughed. "It's moving along slowly. We're looking for a cook or chef to create our baked goods. We've also started to look around for a bakery location."

"I think your idea is a fabulous one. It's going to take off like wildfire!" Shirley said.

"Thank you, my darling Shirl! I appreciate your support."

"Have you considered perhaps doing more than selling from a counter?"

"What do you mean?" She had him curious now.

"Well, think about having a small cafe at the front. You could serve the baked goods you make, as well as some non-cannabis laced ones. People will get the munchies after enjoying some of your products. They'll want to eat something, or bring snacks home to eat afterward, you get where I'm going with this? What do seniors love the most?"

"Going out for coffee." PopPop ventured a guess.

"Exactly! They would come to your bakery, have a regular coffee and cinnamon bun, buy some to go, and also buy some of your laced scotch mints or pudding for later on."

"Shirley, my dear, you have a brilliant business mind! I'll have to introduce you to George!"

Chapter 14

Ashley was waiting nervously for a table at Chez Henri's. She kind of wished that Tasha had been on shift this evening. Maybe having someone she knew might have eased her anxiety about seeing Chef Mackenzie again and the possibility of starting some kind of relationship. Then again, Sophia was right. Tasha would have been lurking around every corner, trying to find out how things were going. That would have added to her anxiety. There was no alternative but to face her nervousness head-on and overcome it.

"Ashley?" It was Chef Mac. He had come out of the kitchen to greet her.

"Good evening, Chef Mac."

"Please, call me Mac," he said. "I have a good feeling that we might become friends, so let's drop the formalities, shall we?"

'He's a smooth one,' Ashley thought. 'I'd sure like us to become more than friends.'

What she said out loud instead was, "Of course. Thank you for coming out to greet me."

"No, thank you for coming to my restaurant tonight. I'll prepare you La Caille, and a few extra special things for the evening."

"You don't have to go out of your way for me." Ashley smiled, looking at him from lowered lashes.

"Oh no, such a beautiful woman needs to be treated to beautiful food." He took her arm in his and walked her to a corner table.

"Unfortunately, I am busy in the kitchen at the moment. I'll join you for coffee and dessert afterward. That's if you don't mind my company?"

"Not at all! I'd love your company. It would be a treat in itself to enjoy dessert with the chef who created it."

"Then it's a date!" His smile melted away any anxiety she might have had left.

AFTER DINNER, TRUE to his word, Chef Mackenzie joined her for coffee and dessert. He brought out a bottle of Hennessy Cognac and two snifters.

"My, you're spoiling me tonight!" Ashley enjoyed the attention she was getting. Sophia and Chloe needed an extra special gift for having encouraged her. Never in a million years had she expected that they would be the ones giving her dating advice.

"You obviously are a woman of great taste. I thought you should finish the evening properly."

"This Cognac is exactly what is called for after a fantastic dinner. Truly, you are a very talented individual."

"You flatter me." He reached out for her hand.

"Are you working late tonight?" she asked, her eyes mischievously sparkling.

"Unfortunately, I have to close. We're short-staffed. Even our dishwasher called in sick."

"You're going to be doing the dishes?" She was surprised that such a talented chef wouldn't have someone to do this work for him, yet she was also impressed that he wasn't too full of himself to do so.

"That's the down part of being the owner of the restaurant you work at. When staff bails on you, you're stuck holding the dishrag."

"Oh, I forgot to mention, the auction started yesterday."

"I know, I've already placed a bid." He crossed his fingers. "Wish me luck. I signed up for the notice as soon as you sent me the link. I got the email with the start time."

"Fingers crossed! I'm sorry that I can't do anything about it," Ashley said. "It's now in the hands of the auction house, and one of my colleagues looks after our auctions. I can't step on her toes."

"I don't expect any special favors. At least not regarding the auction." His words made Ashley blush. "You will be getting a lot of bidders on it."

"I certainly hope so."

"I guarantee you that the last owner, Chef Damon Archer, will bid. With what money, I have no idea? Watch out for this guy, he's quick to anger and could harass you."

"You should have warned me sooner. He's already paid me a visit." Ashley took a sip of cognac. "Don't worry, we took care of him. I don't think he will be paying me another visit anytime soon."

"Damn. He's not the only one who will bid, though. There's this German chef, Gunther Wolf, who is a huge fan of anything that Chef Akira Wataru touched."

"That makes me happy to hear. The more who bid, the better."

"For you perhaps, unfortunately not for me." He raised his glass to her. "And there's another one who will definitely not want to miss this auction."

"What's his name?"

"Chef François is the name he goes by now. A total whack job. Nice guy, but quite crazy in the head. He thinks he's..."

"Chef Akira Wataru." She finished for him. "Oh crap, you already met him." He laughed.

"So, what's the deal with him? Other than thinking he's a dead chef of course."

"He's a volatile person and a bit deluded. He was an up-and-coming force to be reckoned with in the industry. Everyone said he was going to be the next Alain Ducasse, but rather than being a French chef, he would be the American version of Ducasse."

"I take it that didn't work for him?"

"No, he crashed and burned. He started partying a bit too much, started believing his own press and thought he didn't have to work for it anymore." He tsked as he thought back on Chef François' history. "When things went sideways for him, he became known as someone who couldn't be relied on, someone who didn't always show up and often produced less than stellar dishes, and he just cracked."

"Cracked?" Ashley asked.

"Yes, he started calling himself Chef François and took on a French accent. He was telling anyone who would listen that the problem he had with his dishes and why he was blackballed was because he had crappy knives. If he had only had better tools, he would have lived up to his potential."

"Oh my."

"Yeah, he began collecting knives from as many well-known chefs as possible," he went on. "He would buy a new set, then declare he was back, better than ever. Of course, he wasn't and so he would go in search of the next set."

"And so that's why he wants this set so badly?" Ashley asked.

"Yes."

"Do you know him personally?"

"We've met a few times, but I try to stay away as much as possible. His delusions are a bit toxic and he's a bit volatile."

"Are all chefs a bit disturbed?"

"I wouldn't say we're 'disturbed'," he replied with a devilish smile. "We are more like very in touch with our emotions and dedicated to our craft. Maybe a tad more than the average person. That's why we might fly off the handle a bit."

"Should I be worried about spending time with you then, Mac?" Ashley teased.

"Not at all. We reserve this lack of diplomacy to the kitchen. Someone like you can expect different emotions."

Ashley thought she might swoon.

"THANKS FOR LETTING me come over so late and unannounced, Mads."

"If I had a guy in here, I wouldn't have let you in." Maddy grinned. "As you can see, there's not a single guy in here, much to my disappointment."

"You could have a guy in here if you wanted to."

"I know, it's just that I haven't met anyone that I'd like to invite upstairs for a nightcap."

"I'll have to do then."

"Yep, you'll have to. What's in that takeout box you're holding?" Maddy had noticed a large restaurant takeaway container in Ashley's arms.

"This little box? It's just dessert from Chez Henri's. That's all."

"That's all? Are the contents shareable?"

"Yes."

"What are you waiting for? Let's get some forks!"

"I thought you might appreciate dessert. I was too full after dinner to eat mine. Mac was kind enough to send two home with me after I mentioned how I knew you would love the dessert menu."

"Mac? As in Chef Mackenzie?"

"Yes, the one and the same."

"Am I to infer from the use of a diminutive that things went well tonight?" Maddy asked.

"Yes, they went very well, actually..." Adding hesitantly, "I think?"

"Well, which is it? Either it went very well or not. You can't end with 'I think?' " Maddy took the dessert-filled box from her and placed it on her glass dining room table.

113

Ashley bit her lower lip and sat at the table, facing the window. "He flirted with me, there's no doubt about it. He called me beautiful and said I deserved beautiful food. He also teased me about showing me certain emotions."

"Certain emotions? What kind of emotions was he referring to?"

"He didn't specify. You had to be there. I'm pretty sure they weren't the kind one experiences in a restaurant."

"That sounds very positive and downright smooth. I want me some of those 'emotions.'" Maddy grabbed two forks and plates from a cupboard, brought them over, and sat down facing Ashley. She opened the box and found two identical meringue Pavlovas covered with fresh blackberries, pomegranates, and groundberries. "Talk about beautiful. These look like a cloud covered in sparkling jewels. Is that gold leaf on top of them?"

"It looks like it. They are lovely looking. Almost too nice to eat," Ashley said, admiring the perfectly round desserts. She lifted one out of the box and gingerly placed it on one of the plates.

"Almost, but not for me!" Maddy dug into hers without placing it on her plate and laughed. Then she lifted it out of the box and put it on the plate in front of her. "Okay, don't look at me like that. I do have manners after all. It just looked too yummy to wait." They both laughed.

"Okay, hon, now tell me, what makes you doubt his interest in you?" Maddy asked.

"It could be me. After I left, I went over our conversation. He told me to call him 'Mac.'"

"And? That's good, no?"

"Yes, and then he added that it was because he felt that we were becoming friends." Ashley looked down, a bit sad. "I wouldn't mind exploring this friendship and seeing if it could go a little further."

"What exactly did he say?"

"He said, and I quote, well more or less quote 'I have a feeling we might become friends' and 'Let's drop the formalities.'" She took a bite of Pavlova. "I'm so confused. After all the smooth talking and flirting this evening, he didn't even try to kiss me goodbye after dinner or even hug me.

"From that, you deduced that he only wanted to be friends?" Maddy was incredulous. Ashley was a beautiful and unbelievably intelligent woman, but when it came to men, she was insecure. It made no sense whatsoever to Maddy as men seemed to flock to her friend like bees to a flower. Then again, her friend had so much dysphoria-related anxiety that it sometimes clouded her mind. She managed to hide it from most people. Maddy knew that underneath Ashley's bravado was a woman who struggled with her body image. It was in situations like this that it hurt her to see how much Ashley still struggled, even after all these years. Maddy needed to remind herself to give her best friend some grace and understanding.

"Do you want my opinion?"

"Yes, please."

"I think he was being flirty while also being respectful, but not too respectful."

"Respectful? How?"

"By not being presumptuous about your future relationship, if there could be one." Maddy smiled. "He wants to get to know you. He probably doesn't want to scare you off by saying straight out that he wanted to be more than friends. He made it clear through flirting. Obvious flirting, according to your description of this evening. Did you tell him you wanted to be more than friends?"

"Of course not, that would be..."

"Presumptuous," Maddy finished Ashley's sentence."Tonight was all about testing the waters."

"Okay, I see what you mean. I'm lacking confidence in myself, I guess."

"That's alright. We all do when it comes to dating from time to time. You're allowed to as well, Miss Perfection."

"Enough about my social life. Do you have any wine hiding somewhere around here?" Ashley appeared to be feeling better. "Not only do I have some wine, I have Inniskillin Vidal ice wine." Maddy got up to get a bottle out of the fridge.

"What? Why didn't you bring that out the minute I walked in the door?"

Maddy poured them both a generous amount, sat back at the table, leaned forward, and raised her glass to Ashley's.

"Here's to the men we love, and here's to the men who love us. But the men we love aren't the men who love us, so the hell with men, and here's to us!"

Chapter 15

SUNDAY

"Maddy, I'm at the police station. I need help. Now!" Ashley's voice on Maddy's phone's voicemail sounded scared and trembling. Maddy had never heard Ashley sound so rattled.

When Ashley's call had arrived, Maddy was finishing a grilled cheese sandwich stuffed with pickles she had prepared herself for brunch. PopPop had taught her to make them like that when she was little. Zane was on the line chatting away about seeing Ryan the Gosling off. He was really a gander, but it was more fun to call him that than 'Ryan Gander'. She quickly ended her call with Zane, unfortunately, she had not been fast enough to pick up Ashley's call. So, Ashley had left a message. Maddy hoped it was more good news regarding the knives. It turned out to be anything but.

She tried to call Ashley back, needing more information. Her call went immediately to voicemail. Hoping beyond hope that she had meant the downtown police station, Maddy grabbed her keys and rushed out the door.

She arrived at the police station and ran to the front desk. Much to her chagrin, it was Officer Kowalchuk who was there, staring at his computer. She suspected that he was probably playing solitaire. Officer Stanley Kowalchuk was not her favorite member of the men in blue. He was cocky, rude, and arrogant, and worst of all, as far as Maddy was concerned, he was lazy. She had had a few run-ins with the constable in the past. He had often been unhelpful and, in some cases, had even proven to have taken actions that had endangered people. He had been appropriately reprimanded by his higher-ups, but Maddy didn't forget and forgive easily, not in this case, no matter how hard she tried.

"Hi, Kowalchuk," she greeted him, trying to catch her breath. He took his time pulling his eyes off the screen and directed his gaze toward her. "Would Ashley Mueller happen to be here?"

"Oh, Yes! Yes, she is," he abruptly stood up. "Come this way."

He quickly buzzed her through and opened up the back door that led to their offices.

"I'll let them know you're here," he said as he rushed back to the front desk.

'Oh shit, Kowalchuk's being uber nice,' Maddy thought. 'It must be worse than I thought.'

Detective Kyle O'Brady came out of a far-end office to her left. He hurried down the hallway and was next to her in mere seconds.

"What's going on, Kyle?" Maddy asked. "I got a voicemail from Ashley asking for help. Why? Where is she?"

Maddy immediately felt somewhat reassured to find Kyle at work today. He was a former boyfriend of Ashley's, and they had remained good friends. His love for Ashley was an emotion he never really tried to hide.

"She's in an interrogation room being questioned, and no one's telling me anything. They know we're friends, so they're keeping me at arm's length."

"You have no idea?"

"No. None whatsoever. People were scurrying up and down the halls, avoiding me like the plague. I have no idea where they were going or what's happening. I'm walking up to people who are having conversations, and they immediately stop talking. I don't like this one bit. Not. One. Bit. Maddy!"

"You aren't helping ease my mind, Kyle," Maddy said. "I'm getting very anxious. Even Kowalchuk's acting strange."

They stood in the hallway, waiting for something to happen. Finally, a door opened, and Sergeant Rafik Kumar came into the hallway.

"Sarge!" Kyle said. "What's going on?"

"Detective." Kumar nodded in his direction. "Ms. Whitman, we keep meeting under the most unfortunate circumstances."

"We do?" She had met him some time ago when she had been questioned about the death of a man. It turned out he was, unfortunately, the first victim of a serial killer. But why were today's circumstances unfortunate? Her palms began to sweat, and she took a deep breath in an attempt to slow her breathing.

"Is Ashley okay?" Kyle interjected, not wanting to waste precious time with chitchat.

"Yes, she's fine. We have her in for questioning regarding a recent homicide."

"Homicide?" Maddy was confused. 'What on earth could Ashley have to do with a homicide?' She wondered.

"Come into my office," Kumar nodded in the direction of an office at the opposite end of the hallway that Kyle had come from. They walked there in silence, Maddy glancing over at Kyle. He looked serious and stressed, which freaked her out even more. His jaw was clenched, his brow furrowed, and he seemed paler than usual. Maddy wondered what on earth could be going on.

Sergeant Kumar sat down behind his big desk and asked them to take a seat.

"Earlier today, a dead body was reported. We have every reason to believe it was a homicide, probably a cold-blooded murder. We think Ashley may be somehow involved or know something about it."

"Wait a minute, let's start at the beginning. First of all, are you sure it was murder?" Kyle asked.

"Well, there was a knife sticking out of his heart," Kumar deadpanned.

"Why are you interrogating Ashley?" Maddy cut in. Enough talk about the dead person, she wanted to know what was going on with her friend.

"Ashley's name was in the calendar of the deceased, along with her office phone number."

"So?" Maddy asked.

"And there are eyewitnesses who report having seen her with him on the day he died. She had visited with him previously to show him some knives. That's pretty suspicious considering the murder weapon found at the scene."

"I can see you wanting to talk to her, but why bring her downtown and put her in an interrogation room?" Kyle asked.

"Yeah, she sounded petrified on the voicemail she left me," Maddy said.

"It was her knife that killed him," Kumar informed them.

Both Maddy's and Kyle's eyes widened in shock. Of all the things they had expected him to say, this had not even crossed their minds.

"Her knife," Kyle muttered. It wasn't a question; it was a disbelieving statement. "How do you know it was her knife?"

"Because she said she had an appointment a few days earlier to show someone there a set of knives, then decided to go back to the restaurant for dinner. We asked her to show us the roll of knives. When she did, one of the knives was missing." Kumar stated. "That's when the detectives on the case decided to bring her into the station for questioning." Sergeant Kumar folded his hands on his desk.

"I shouldn't have told you this much. I'm only sharing this information out of respect for you, Detective. I know Ms. Mueller is a close friend."

Knives? Roll? Maddy became nauseated. It wasn't possible that Ashley had another set of knives she was carrying around, was it?

"I think those knives are mine," Maddy said.

"What?" Sergeant Kumar practically shouted as he sprang out of his chair. "Why didn't Ms. Mueller tell us that? She said she was selling them for a client of hers."

"I am that client, and she's selling them for me!"

"When was the last time you saw those knives?" The sergeant sat back down and leaned forward over his desk, staring intently at Maddy.

"Sometime last week, when we agreed she would sell them. I went into her office and spoke with her and her colleague about them," Maddy explained. "I left them with her so she could have them professionally photographed."

"I'll need the name of her colleague so we can verify your story," Kumar said.

"Joshua Hampton," Maddy said.

"Sarge, the knife that was missing, how do you know it is the same one missing from Maddy's collection?" Kyle asked. Maddy noticed how he made sure to remind the Sargent that the knives belonged to her, not Ashley. Not that it surprised her. If faced with the possibility of 'his' Ashley being in trouble or Maddy being in trouble, she knew he would throw her to the wolves, every single time. He wouldn't like it, but he would do it.

"We are looking into that now. It appears the knife found in his chest is the missing knife. We've had visual confirmation from Ms. Mueller, and we will be comparing them to the photos that Ms. Whitman mentioned. The photographer is getting the proofs over to us today. We're also comparing the fingerprints. We already have hers and yours from your last visit with a certain African mask."

"It was Mexican, from Mazatlán," Maddy corrected him.

"That's not important, Maddy," Kyle whispered to her, noticing that the sergeant was starting to look frustrated.

"Detective O'Grady, please stay away from this investigation unless we ask you. At least until we can rule Ms. Mueller out. From what I've

121

found out so far, it won't take too long. We cannot look like we gave your friend any preferential treatment, got it?

"Yes, Sir. I understand."

They were on their way out of the sergeant's office when something suddenly occurred to Maddy. "Excuse me, Sergeant Kumar?"

"Yes, Ms. Whitman?"

"Who was killed?"

"Davis," he replied, as he closed his door behind them.

THEY DID NOT BOTHER with interrogating Maddy at the station since she had not been the last person in possession of the knives and was not considered a suspect. Instead, she was asked to make a statement about where she found the knives and when she had last seen the complete set.

"There," Maddy signed the bottom of her statement with a flourish. "I've written everything I could about these knives. When will I be able to take Ashley home?"

"Her lawyer just showed up," Kyle said. "It probably won't be long, once someone brings in a lawyer, it usually ends talks pretty quickly. And from what I have been told, she has already told the detectives everything they needed to know. A couple of times by the sounds of it."

"I'll just wait here then."

"I have to get back and work on some of my cases. Please, please keep me posted, okay?" Kyle asked. "Ashley should stay with you tonight. I'd like to accompany you both home when you're done here, if you don't mind? I can slip out early today."

"Sure." He was such a nice guy, Maddy thought. When he and Ashley had briefly dated, they hit it off. Then things had started getting too serious for her friend's liking. She wasn't ready to settle down and broke things off with Kyle. It was obvious to anyone who knew him that he still held a torch for her. Maddy was just grateful that he was still willing to be around when things like this happened to her or one of her friends. She could not imagine how difficult it would be navigating things if they did not have Kyle on their side.

"Oh damn, Zane!" Speaking of nice guys they knew, she had forgotten all about him. She grabbed her cell and tapped his number in. They were supposed to go for one last visit with Ryan, and now she would have to cancel. There was no way she was going to just go about her day as though her friend might not need her.

"Hey, I'm afraid I have to cancel my visit with you to go see Ryan today," she told him when he answered.

"Oh," he said, then fell silent on the other end.

"I'm sorry to leave it so late," Maddy said. "There's a critical situation with Ashley. I'm at the police station right now."

"Police station? Is everyone okay?" he asked, voice tinged with worry.

"Yeah, well, no. Someone was killed. A chef. And they brought Ashley in for questioning. She's the last person they are aware of who had the murder weapon that was used to kill him," Maddy explained. "Plus, she was seen with him just hours before he was found dead."

"They're interrogating her? Does she have a lawyer with her?"

"Yes, he's with her now. Kyle found one for her," Maddy replied. "I feel responsible because the weapon came from my knife collection."

"The fancy one you told me about?"

"Yeah, one of the knives is missing, and they think it's the one found sticking out of the chef's body."

"Whoa, that's nasty. So, you're the knives' owner. They would want to ask you questions. Have they talked to you yet?"

"Yes, I gave them a statement," Maddy said.

"Did you have your lawyer present with you?" By the tone of his voice, she suspected it was a loaded question.

"No, there was no need. They only wanted me to write out when I saw them last and stuff."

"Maddy! Never, ever give a statement to the police about a serious crime without your lawyer's knowledge! It doesn't matter how innocuous it seems, you have to have legal representation. If you're ever in that situation again, if they ask you to come back in for more questioning, or something similar, please call me. I know several criminal lawyers, and I'd be able to help you out."

Maddy was afraid to ask how he had such an intimate understanding of the law and why he knew so many criminal lawyers. Was her spikey-haired friend keeping something from her? Did he have a dark and dangerous past he had neglected to tell her about? Tasha was right. How well did she know him? 'Stop it!' she told herself. 'Your imagination is running away with you.'

"Listen, Maddy, don't stress about not visiting Ryan. We can do that another day, okay? Try not to over-worry. We both know she didn't do it." He tried to reassure her. "Remember, it's 'Innocent until proven guilty', right?

"Right."

"Why don't I bring the donuts and meet you at your place when you guys get back from the station? I can help figure out what to do next, okay?"

"That would be appreciated. I'm sure Ashley hasn't eaten anything today."

"I'll pick up some bagels and cream cheese instead, then, and see you soon."

"Thanks. Umm... Zane?"

"Yes, Maddy?"

"Can you still bring donuts, please? We'll need them for comfort after the bagels."

Chapter 16

"My lawyer advised me that since I told the detectives everything I knew and that, unless they planned on arresting me, I shouldn't say anything further," Ashley explained to Maddy, Zane, and Kyle as she sat on Maddy's couch sipping tea and devouring another donut from the Donut Party store.

"That's good advice," Zane said, nodding in agreement. "From what you've said, they know enough to continue with their investigation. They know who the knife belongs to, and they know you weren't anywhere near the restaurant after you left yesterday evening. Once they narrow down the time of death, they will probably want to know where you were then. I would recommend that, while it is still fresh, you write down exactly where you were and at what time. That way you're prepared." He walked over to Maddy's large picture window and stood on one side of it.

"Is all that necessary?" Maddy asked. "Surely they don't seriously think it could be her."

"It doesn't matter; she needs to protect herself," Zane asserted.

Kyle turned and scowled at him. "The police aren't the enemy, they aren't out to get her," he said through clenched teeth.

"That's fine, however, she still needs to protect herself, and the first step in that is realizing the police aren't her friends," Zane said. "I know you are Kyle, and I respect that, but your view might be a bit biased for that very reason."

"Really? So do tell us what your opinions are colored by?" Kyle retorted. Maddy could have sworn he puffed out his chest toward Zane.

"Okay, enough, enough," Maddy stepped between them. "We're all upset, and we all want what's best for Ashley. There's no use arguing amongst ourselves."

The men glared at each other and then went to sit down, each picking a bean bag on opposite sides. Maddy could have sworn they were pouting.

"They told me not to leave town," Ashley said. "I thought they only said that in the movies."

"They say that to everyone, don't worry about it," Kyle said while looking at Zane defiantly.

"I have work to do, I travel a lot," Ashley started pacing Maddy's living room. "There's this international conference that I must attend in Chicago in two weeks. How am I supposed to go if I can't leave town?"

"Let's take things one step at a time, Ash," Maddy reassured her. "I'm sure something can be arranged. For now, why don't we try to figure out who had access to the knife?"

"Good idea, Maddy," Kyle said, turning to Ashley. "Who has been alone with the knife roll or that knife in particular?"

"I don't know, I don't think there was anyone..."

"What about the photographer?" Maddy asked.

"Yes! But he's an old man who still uses film, I can't see him knifing someone. And anyway, why?" Ashley looked thoughtful.

"Did you see the complete set after the pics were taken?" Kyle asked her.

"Yes, I did. I took the knife roll to show them after, and they were all there."

"Okay, now anyone else?" Kyle prodded her to think back. "Did anyone else have access?"

"Paris did, we accidentally exchanged carryall bags because they're identical," Ashley said. "She had it overnight, and to be honest, I didn't check it when she returned it."

"Okay, that's good, now who else?" Zane leaned forward in his seat.

"Well, I guess pretty much anyone who was at the restaurant when I went there the first time. I left it at the table when I went into the kitchen to watch Mac, I mean Chef Mac, prepare a dish. Then I accidentally left my bag with the roll in it behind. That means the chef himself, the sous-chefs, maybe a waiter or two. Oh, and of course, Tasha." Ashley smiled at the idea of Tasha being considered a suspect.

"What about that crazy guy, the one who thinks you should give him the knives?" Zane asked.

"Damon Archer? I don't think he was left alone with them. I certainly wouldn't have felt comfortable doing that, given his feelings about the knives," Ashley said.

"So, you know for sure he would have had no opportunity? He doesn't have to have been left alone with them. Even an opportunity to slide one into his pocket or up his sleeve?" Kyle asked.

"I didn't take them out in front of him. I suppose I can't say for 100 percent." Ash looked doubtful.

"Then let's add him to the list anyway," Kyle said. "So, we have Paris, the sous-chefs, a couple of waiters at Chez Henri's restaurant, Tasha, and Damon Archer. Anyone else?"

"I don't think so," Ashley said.

"For now, but don't stop thinking about it, Ashley. Something might come back later. You could remember someone else," Zane said.

"So those are the people with the potential means to kill the chef," Kyle said. "Now we need to talk about those who might have had the opportunity."

"Tasha shouldn't even be on that list," Maddy said, looking at everyone. "She hasn't been on the job for more than a couple of weeks, and she loves it. Tasha hasn't stopped talking about how great Chef

Mackenzie is and how he shares leftovers with the staff. " She stopped and looked a bit embarrassed. "I mean 'was' great and 'shared' leftovers."

"She probably is innocent, Maddy," Zane replied. "Still, the detectives have to include her on the possible suspect list until they compare prints and check her alibi."

"Zane's right," added Kyle. "They've probably already called her in. They've likely called in all the staff and any other diners who were there last night. Let's focus on opportunity, shall we?"

"What does that mean exactly?" Ashley asked. "Wouldn't those who had access to the knife be the ones with the opportunity?"

"No, they had the means of committing the crime because they had access to the knife. Those who had the opportunity are those who could have been at the restaurant when he was killed", Zane explained.

"How on earth will we know that?" Maddy spoke up. "If we knew who was there, then we would know who killed him."

"Yes and no. Some people, like Paris and Damon Archer, are unknowns," Kyle said. "Others, like the waiters and sous-chefs, and Tasha, we know they were there when the knife may have disappeared. There's also the patrons eating there, like Ashley, on the evening of the murder itself. Then there's the motive."

"Although, legally, we don't need someone to have a motive, but it's helpful," Zane said, then shrugged when Kyle stared hard at him.

"So anyway, do you know if any of them had a reason to want Mackenzie Davis dead?" Kyle asked Ashley.

"I can't see the people from work having a reason. As for Paris, I have no idea if she even knew him. The others? I'm not acquainted with the employees of Chez Henri's. Damon Archer? Perhaps he thought Chef Mackenzie was going to be his competition and stand in his way to buy back the knives in the auction? Honestly, I'm guessing here." Ashley looked around the room with uncertainty.

"I'm going to see if there have been any developments," Kyle pulled out his cell phone and walked into the kitchen.

"Didn't you tell me that Tasha mentioned Chef Mackenzie was acquainted with Archer?" Maddy asked.

"I believe she did say so, yes. Ugh! I can't believe we're embroiled in another murder," Ashley said, shaking her head. "Every time we turn around, we get pulled into some kind of dangerous situation."

"Well, unlike the time that crazy woman was tying people up in boxes or when George's wife was kidnapped, the police will be involved smack dab in the middle of this one, from the get-go," Maddy said. "Whether we want them to or not."

"Rick's still in Vegas, at least he'll be happy to hear that we're working with the police and not putting his wife in danger," Ashley smiled.

Kyle returned to the group and placed his cellphone on the coffee table.

"They ran the fingerprints that were on the knife. They matched them to Maddy's, Ashley's, and Mackenzie Davis'. There's one other set of prints they found that didn't match anyone. They still don't have Damon Archer's or Paris's or any of the other employees' prints yet," Kyle told them. "Tasha's the only one who has stopped by to be fingerprinted so far, you'll be happy to know that she's not a match. They haven't been able to reach all the restaurant staff. Tasha provided them with a phone list when she came in. They usually give people 24 hours to come in once they have contacted them. They're also checking for touch DNA, that's going to take a bit longer."

"When are they going to get the fingerprints of everyone else?" Ashley asked.

"They're going to call your office and ask people to volunteer to provide their prints," Kyle said. "They'll get to those next, I'm not sure when."

"You're not sure when? I have a conference in two weeks!" Ashley said. "Those unidentified prints could belong to the killer, this could be what solves the case."

"I know, Ashley, but we only have so many resources," Kyle said. "They'll work as fast as they possibly can."

"We know they will, Kyle," Maddy said. "We're just anxious about all of this."

"I completely understand. Maddy, you have to let the police do their work and go about your regular lives, okay?" Kyle said. "I promise to keep you up to date."

"Has anyone spoken with Tasha?" Ashley asked. "I would have thought she'd come here right after the police station."

'Let me try," Maddy called her. "It went straight to voicemail. I'll text her to give us a call asap."

"WHAT DO YOU MEAN YOUR chef was murdered?" Rick asked in disbelief.

"Murdered," Tasha replied. "Stabbed right through the cuore!"

"The what?"

"The heart! Dio mio, what a nightmare."

"Ya Allah! Were you there, habibti?"

"No, thankfully, it was on my night off."

"Thank God."

"That's not all."

"More?" Rick dreaded whatever news was coming next. "They've arrested Ashley!"

"They what?" Rick sat down and stared at his cell. This is not what he wanted to hear during his call.

"No, not arrested. Sorry. They brought her in for questioning. I spoke with Maddy earlier today. She doesn't know much other than it has to do with those knives she found."

"I can't believe it! Ash would never kill someone unless it was in self-defense."

"I don't think they believe that she did it, but she was seen with Mackenzie Davis earlier in the evening. That's why they had questions for her."

"That's a relief."

"They asked the staff to come into the station to answer questions and get fingerprinted to rule us out. They're trying to figure out the timeline. I think it's probably to figure out the time of death and whatnot."

"You have to go in? Do you want me to come home?" Rick grabbed his suitcase and started putting clothes into it.

"No, no. I'm good. I already went in and everything. I have an alibi, and I never touched Maddy's knives." Tasha didn't want her husband missing any important presentations or the opportunity to expand his business network. "Anyway, I'm driving to the restaurant now to do an inventory and call patrons to cancel their reservations. The restaurant has to be closed for a few days."

"I think you need to start taking Karate lessons with the girls."

"Oh, Rick, don't worry. That self-defense course you made me take with Ash and Maddy was more than enough." Tasha said. "Hey, I'd better let you go, I missed a call from Maddy. I should call her back in case she has news about Ash."

"Please let me know what's going on, okay? I hate being so far from you with all this craziness happening around you."

"I will."

"Promise?"

"I promise. Love you!"

"DIO MIO MADDY, IT'S crazy around here," Tasha said, calling from her work. She was talking to her friends who were still gathered at Maddy's. Tasha was relating to them what was going on by way of the speaker on Maddy's cell phone. They wanted to get more details about what had gone on at the restaurant.

"We're all shocked, and no one knows what to do. One of the staff had come in before everyone else to get an early start on food prep this morning and found Chef Mackenzie dead on the kitchen floor," she told them. "The rest of the staff have started trickling in and found the police tape and the poor guy who found Chef being interrogated. He was in total shock. If we weren't trying to console him, we were trying to figure out what had happened. It's been like a game of Clue around here."

"We know it was with a knife in the kitchen, but we can't figure out who it was? Who would want Chef dead?" Have you come up with any ideas?" Ashley asked.

"Everyone is guessing, and so far, the most likely suspects are the garbage man and the guy who supplies us with quail." Tasha sighed. "So, in other words, no. I went to the station earlier and gave my fingerprints. I was home with the girls last night. It was my night off, so I have an alibi."

"Kyle reassures us that they're working the case and following all leads," Maddy said. "Of course, they have limited resources."

"That's what worries me," Tasha said. "The murderer is still on the loose."

The friends went quiet, each thinking about the murder, wondering what had happened and how it would be solved.

"You know..." Maddy began. "I'm thinking..."

"Me too," said Ashley.

"What?" Zane looked from each woman to the other, frowning. "You aren't thinking about getting involved, are you?

"No, not involved," Maddy said. "Don't be silly!"

"Yeah, Zane, you're being ridiculous," Ashley laughed.

Kyle looked at them, not convinced. He then looked at Zane, who was giving him a 'What are they up to now?' look.

"What are you thinking?" Tasha asked.

"Well, if the police have resource issues and they can't get to all the employees at the restaurant, Tasha," Maddy said. "Then maybe we could talk to your coworkers and encourage them to go give their prints today instead of waiting until tomorrow."

"Why?" Tasha asked. "They already asked us all to go in and get our prints taken."

"Kyle said they don't have the time to go chasing every individual employee to get prints, so they're waiting for them to come in. If we can get them to come in a bit faster, maybe by giving them rides to the station, it might help the detectives narrow things down faster. They can start eliminating them as suspects more quickly. Then they can focus on the ones who don't show up and figure out what they're hiding."

"Not wanting to give your fingerprints isn't always because you're hiding," Zane spoke up. "Sometimes it is a privacy issue, and sometimes it is just simply an expression of their rights."

"Yes, and that's exactly what the police are for," Ashley said. "We provide them with the information on those who don't want to come in, and they figure out what to do with it."

"Tasha, would you be able to give us the list you gave the police of all the employees who work at Chez Henri's?" Maddy asked.

"Sure, no problem. I'll send it to you as soon as possible. I just arrived at the restaurant." Tasha said. "I'll go to the back of the kitchen and call you when I get there. There's a more detailed list of all the employees the manager keeps on the wall. I should send it to the detectives, too. I'm sure I missed a name or two when they asked me. Anyway, I'll get it and text you a pic so you can get started on calling to offer rides."

"Perfect, Tasha, we'll wait," Ashley said. "Maddy, let's work on a script of how we will approach them and then split up the list, how does that sound?"

"Works for me," Maddy said.

"You know, ladies, those phone numbers are private information. You can't go around calling people in their homes and strongarming them to go down to the station," Zane said.

"We're not going to strongarm anyone," Maddy replied. "We're going to guilt them."

"I hate to agree with Zane here," Kyle interrupted, "he's right, their phone numbers are private information. Also, and most importantly, don't interfere with the investigation."

"Kyle, come on, we're not going to be interfering. We're only going to offer rides." Maddy gave him her best puppy dog eyes.

Kyle got up and walked to the door. "I have to go. But before I do, please promise me that you are not, and I repeat, NOT going to call anyone. Leave the detective work to the detectives." He left, shaking his head.

"It's my turn to hate to agree with Kyle," Zane said. "He's right. Let the police do their thing. It might take a bit of time, but they will find the murderer. Even if you get all Chez Henri's staff to the station tonight, the prints won't get processed until tomorrow. It's Sunday after all."

"We can't sit around and do nothing, Zane." Ashley was tearing up. "Mac was such a nice guy and talented. I feel helpless sitting around here, waiting for the overworked and understaffed police to get to eventually find the son of a bitch who killed him!"

"Why don't you give the staff their 24 hours? I'm sure that if they don't show up by then, the police will contact them again," Zane suggested. "If that happens, then you start offering rides, and do it through Tasha so none of you are breaking privacy laws, okay?"

"I don't know Zane..." Maddy wasn't convinced but seemed to be mulling it over.

Just then, Ashley's phone dinged with an incoming text, and she grabbed it off the counter.

"Oh my god!" she said.

"What? What is it?" Zane asked.

She turned it around to show the two of them what was on the screen. It was a text from Tasha.

'The murderer is here!'

Chapter 17

"The murderer is here!'

"What the hell!" Zane rushed over to where Ashley was and grabbed her phone out of her hands. While he was staring at the screen, it rang. He answered immediately. "Tasha, what's going on? Tasha?"

He looked at the two women who were now staring at him. "She isn't answering, but I can tell she's on the other end. I can hear moving around," he said. "She could be in danger. Let's not talk to her."

"What do you mean, we shouldn't talk to her?" Maddy asked.

They heard Tasha say something indistinguishable on the other end.

"We don't want the murderer to hear any noise coming from Tasha's phone," Ashley said. "Tasha's a smart cookie. I bet she called us so we can listen in and be witnesses."

"And make sure she's safe," Zane added. "Do you all still have that 'Where's my family' app on your cells?"

"Yes!" Maddy replied, knowing exactly where Zane was going with this.

"Good. Let's see if she needs our help or not. I don't want us to endanger her by making noise."

THE CRIME SCENE TAPE had been removed from the front door. Tasha punched the code into the lock and let herself in. The front of the house in the restaurant seemed eerily quiet. Her mind was probably playing tricks on her. The restaurant was usually quiet when it was empty, and no staff were around. Just knowing someone had been killed there was causing her to shiver.

She made her way between the tables, cell phone in hand, to find a copy of the employees' shift schedules by the back kitchen door. It was intended for Chez Henri's employees to be able to access other employees in case someone wanted to call and switch shifts.

Approaching the kitchen door, she heard people speaking and hesitated. It was obvious that an argument was taking place. Voices were raised, and a heated exchange was happening behind the closed double swing door. Should she just go in and interrupt them? Pretend she didn't hear anything? She was pondering what to do next when the exchange turned into yelling, and she could hear every word they were saying as clearly as if she were in the kitchen with them.

"I did it for you!" one voice shouted.

"When I said I could 'kill' him, I didn't mean it literally! It was a figure of speech, you moron!" the other voice shouted back.

"How the hell was I supposed to know that, eh?" the first voice retorted.

"BECAUSE KILLING SOMEONE IS A CRIME!" The second voice was fast becoming unhinged.

"Well, sooorry for trying to do you a favor! Now what do we do?"

"We? There's no 'we' here. You have to make sure that nobody, and I mean NOBODY, ever finds out what happened." The second voice sounded threatening.

Tasha's mouth went dry. Chef Mackenzie's killer was here! She was frozen in place for a few seconds before she opened the texting feature on her phone and sent Ashley a message. She called her and put her hand on the speaker. She didn't dare say anything to her friends or let their voices come through. She couldn't risk either of the two in the kitchen hearing any sounds coming from her direction.

Tasha heard the kitchen's outer back door open and shut with a bang. Slowly opening the kitchen door, she peered in. No one was in the kitchen. They both must have left. She hurried over to the door, hoping to get a glimpse of the killer. She saw a car pulling out of the parking lot, tires squealing, a late-model red Toyota Corolla. Squinting her eyes, she was barely able to make out the license plate. Buffalo, giant, panda 24-17 - Buffalo, giant, panda, 24-17 she repeated over and over in her head. Suddenly, she remembered that her friends were still on the line and lifted her cell to her ear.

"Write this down, buffalo, giant, panda 24-17," she said. She heard Zane repeating her words to Ashley and Maddy.

"What's going on, Tasha?"

"I'm not sure, I think I just heard one of the sous-chefs talking to someone about having killed Chef Mackenzie."

"Are they still there?"

"No, they've just pulled out of the back parking lot, that's the license plate number I gave you." Even though she hadn't exerted herself, Tasha was breathing heavily. The adrenaline was still coursing through her veins, and her heart was pounding.

"You need to get out of there now, Tasha!" It was Maddy, she had yanked the phone out of Zane's hand. "You don't want to be there in case they come back."

"We need to report this to the police," Tasha said.

"Yes, we will. First, you need to get out of there. How about we meet you at the police station?" Maddy suggested.

"Okay, I had to park a bit of a walk from the restaurant today, but I'll get there as quickly as I can." Tasha hung up the phone and headed to her car as fast as she could.

When she arrived at the restaurant, there had been an event happening in one of the buildings situated nearby, and Tasha had had to park a couple of blocks away. It was now starting to get dark. Tasha picked up her pace, walking swiftly down the sidewalk. As she turned a corner, she could swear she heard footsteps coming from behind, walking quickly toward her. She looked over her shoulder, no one was there. Trying to reassure herself, she repeated over and over, 'You're perfectly safe, you're perfectly safe, don't let your fear and imagination run away on you...'

Who was she kidding? She was nervous because she had heard someone, who she thought might be a restaurant colleague, had killed another co-worker. With a knife no less.

What an awful and brutal way to end someone's life. Knives seemed to be a man's preferred weapon of choice. A woman, on the other hand, would not want to be that up close and personal with whoever she was intent on killing. Unless, of course, it was revenge, then a woman could angrily stab a person repeatedly, over and over, due to blind fury.

'Alright, that's enough!' she told herself. Her thoughts were darting left and right as she worked at steadying her heartbeat. She had just entered the back alley where her car was parked when she took a few steps and abruptly turned around. The sound of another person's steps stopped, and she saw a large shadow move behind a large industrial garbage container.

'Merda', she thought. 'Someone IS following me.'

She turned back around and picked up the pace, hurrying toward her car. Fumbling for her phone, she struggled with it as she continued to flee. In her nervousness, it dropped from her shaking hand. Tasha bent down to pick it up and heard the steps coming closer. Quickly swooping it off the ground, she began running at full speed, giving quick glances at her phone. The pursuer was catching up to her. Tasha could hear his grunts and heavy footsteps as he pushed himself harder. She hit the automatic dial emergency button that linked to Rick's phone number, forgetting that he wasn't in town. Rick cheerfully answered his phone with a "Hi, beautiful!"

Tasha was unable to respond. The man chasing her down the alley had pounced on top of her, placing one hand over her mouth and shoving her to the ground. She hit the packed gravel with an audible thud. The wind being knocked out of her made her gasp loudly. She struggled, trying hard to fight back, but it was impossible to do so while lying face down on the ground. She was kicking and elbowing any part of her aggressor's body that he could reach and was also trying to bite the strong hand over her mouth. Finally, she managed to make contact with her aggressor, and he loosened his grip enough for her to be able to turn her body around.

"Tasha! What's going on? Tasha!" Rick cried out from his Las Vegas hotel room. His imagination was running wild with fear.

The man looked down at her, smiled, and raised his arm high above his head, blocking the streetlight and casting a dark shadow over her face. All she could see was a knife glinting in his hand. She screamed as loudly as her lungs would allow her. "Where are you?" Rick shouted. Then everything went deadly quiet.

"TASHA!"

Chapter 18

Maddy and Ashley were talking incessantly as Zane drove them to the police station, wondering if it could be possible for the murder to have been solved this quickly and easily. Did that car's license plate number belong to one of the killers? Would the police be able to trace the license and act on their tip?

Rick's call interrupted their conversation.

"Should I let him know what we've been up to?" Maddy asked while her phone's ringer played 'Walk Like an Egyptian'.

"Sure," Zane said. "It's pretty much over now."

"I don't know," Ashley replied. "Maybe we should let Tasha tell him."

"Hey there, Mister Rick, how's Vegas been treating you?" she asked.

"Never mind that! Tasha's in trouble! You have to go to her!"

"What? No, don't worry, we talked to her, she gave us a plate number, and she's going to meet us at the police station," Maddy looked at Ashley, who was motioning to fill her in on what Rick was saying. "She's okay, really."

She put him on speakerphone.

"No! No! She called seconds ago. I can't explain right now. Tasha's in trouble, you need to help her! You need to go to her now, as fast as you possibly can." He was yelling through the phone, frustration in his voice that they didn't understand his urgency. "Call 9-1-1 and ask for the police and an ambulance. I'm going to keep trying her cell."

"Rick! Wait! Where is she? Is she near the restaurant?" Maddy asked.

"Close. I'll pin you her location from the 'Where's my family' app.

"That's okay, I can get it off the app. Zane, turn around, we have to find Tasha. Head toward the restaurant where she works," Maddy said, her voice rising as her fear of their friend being in danger grew.

"Where's that?"

"Ashley can tell you. I'm going to open the app and look for her cell phone's exact location. We'll find her, Rick. Don't worry about it, we've got this," Maddy tried to reassure him.

"Thank you, let me know as soon as you find her," Rick said. "I'm never leaving town without her again. I swear it!"

"Hey, we're on it. I promise, we won't leave you hanging any longer than we have to. She's going to be fine."

"I'll call 9-1-1." Ashley was already dialing. "Show me the location."

THEY PULLED IN BEHIND two police cruisers and an ambulance. Flashing lights were bathing the buildings in a wash of red and blue. "Oh my God, oh my God!"

If pressed later, Zane could not have said whether it was Maddy or Ashley, or both of them, who cried out. All three were running toward the center of activity, skirting around anyone who got in their way. Maddy came to a sudden halt when she came upon Tasha's body lying on the ground. She knelt next to her friend's prone form.

"Ma'am, you can't be here," she heard a voice say. "Ma'am!"

"Tasha, oh my God, Tasha. Is she okay?" Maddy asked, turning to the emergency attendant who was pressing down on Tasha's stomach, valiantly trying to stop the bleeding.

"You have to leave now." A hand grabbed hold of her arm, applying pressure. Maddy shook it off.

"S'oh kay, bella," Tasha mumbled quietly through dry lips. Her eyes struggled to focus on Maddy's face. "Girls... Ri..." She couldn't finish her words.

"Don't worry about them, they're okay," Maddy reassured her.

Tasha's eyes glazed over and rolled to the back of her head, then her lids slowly closed. Her breathing appeared to stop. "No Tasha, NO!"

"We'll be taking her to the Royal Alexandra Hospital. You can meet us there," one of the ambulance attendants said gently. "Please, you have to step aside, you're endangering her by not letting us do our job."

"Maddy, hon, come with me. Let them do what they need to do to save her, okay?" This time, it was Ashley who was softly taking Maddy by the arm. She guided her away from Tasha so the emergency crew could continue to work on her as they lifted her onto a stretcher.

The women stayed back until Tasha was safely in the ambulance, and they watched it pull away. As it drove off, its blaring siren sounds were bouncing off buildings around them, adding to their mental anguish.

"Come on, Maddy, let's go," Ashley practically dragged her back toward Zane's car.

"Let's go to the hospital," Ashley told Zane as she opened the car door and pushed Maddy into the front seat. She slid into the backseat as Zane jumped in the car and pulled away from the curb.

"Call Rick and tell him what's happening," Ashley leaned forward, her head between them.

Zane looked over at Maddy, who was staring straight ahead. He caught Ashley's eyes in the rearview mirror.

"Maddy, honey," Ashley gently touched her shoulder.

"Did she die?" Maddy's voice was quiet, and Ashley had to lean forward even further to hear what she was saying. "Did she die in front of me?"

"Maddy, the EMTs were in a hurry to get her to the hospital," Ashley said, her voice forceful as she tried to penetrate the shock that was holding Maddy in its clutches. "They wouldn't have been in a hurry if she were dead."

"But what if..."

"No, Maddy! I'm not going to allow you to go there," Ashley cut her off. "Rick must be going out of his mind. I'll call him myself and let him know what's going on."

Maddy continued to stare straight ahead, her thoughts whirling in her mind, thoughts of everything that could go wrong overtaking all others. She felt Zane's hand cover hers and squeeze. She had not realized how cold her hands were until she felt the warmth of his strong fingers wrapped around hers.

"You okay?" he asked quietly so his voice would not interfere with Ashley's conversation with Rick.

"No," Maddy said.

"She's not dead. They didn't cover her face. Look at me," he said. "She's. Not. Dead."

"She's dying, Zane, and it's all because of me."

IN THE HOSPITAL'S WAITING room, Ashley paced the checkerboard-tiled floor while Maddy sat on a hard plastic chair, staring at the clock.

Looking at her phone, Ashley read something and then looked up to share what she had seen with Zane and Maddy.

"Rick is catching the next available flight. He should be here just after midnight."

"Did you tell him she's in surgery?" Maddy asked. "Yes, he knows."

"And that they'll put guards around her room when she gets out?" Maddy pressed.

"Yes, Maddy. I told him everything we know." Ashley sat down beside her friend and threw an arm around her shoulders.

Maddy jumped up suddenly, her eyes wide with fright. "The girls! Where are her girls?"

"It's okay, Maddy," Ashley said. "They're with their grandmother. Mama Leila is taking good care of them."

"I'm sorry for being a basket case," she said, sitting back down. "I just can't get the picture of her closing her eyes out of my head."

"I know, hon," Ashley began to rub her back. "But she didn't die. It's difficult to operate on a dead person, don't you think?"

Maddy smiled. Ashley gave a quiet laugh at her own poor attempt at a joke.

"Actually, that's how they learn..." They turned to stare at Zane, only to find him smiling back at them. "What? You two are the only ones who can break the tension around here with silliness?"

"Are you family or friends of Natasha Nasser?" A doctor stood in the center of the waiting room's entryway. He had on green scrubs, and his face mask hung loosely around his neck. His face was drawn and grim.

Chapter 19

"Maddy, it's very late. I think you need to take a break and go home for a bit," Zane said. "You heard what the doctor said, it was a long and difficult surgery, however, her prognosis is good."

"Zane, he actually used the words 'guarded optimism,' " Maddy corrected him, tearing up.

"Why don't you both go home? I can wait here for Rick," Ashley said. "If anything at all changes, I'll call you immediately."

"Zane's right, you need some rest." Kyle's voice came from behind them. They swung around in surprise, unaware that he had arrived. "The detectives on the case are arranging round-the-clock security for her," he informed them. "It's obvious that Tasha heard something she wasn't supposed to. We need to protect her and find out what it was that she overheard."

"Do they have any idea who did this to her?" Maddy asked.

"No, until Tasha gains consciousness and can answer some questions, there's not a whole lot more we can do. We've canvassed the stores near where she was attacked, no one saw anything unusual," he answered. "We're in the process of gathering any CCTV we can find. Unfortunately, there aren't many in the back alley, we think there should be a few front door cameras along part of the path she took. Hopefully, some will have footage we can use. We're also trying to figure out which one of the sous-chefs is the one you said she mentioned." Then he turned and spoke directly to Maddy. "I heard through the grapevine that you had quite the shock." He glanced at Ashley. "You really should go home and get some rest. As Ashley said, we will let you know if anything changes."

"I'll drive you home," Zane said.

"I'll leave once Rick arrives." The set of Maddy's jaw told them how minuscule their chances were of changing her mind.

"Fine, fine," Ashley threw her arms up in defeat. "I understand how you feel. Can you at least sit down and try to rest a bit? Close your eyes. I promise you won't miss a thing. I'll wake you. Promise." Ashley was as exhausted as her friend, but this shocking experience seemed to have hit Maddy harder than the rest of them. She wondered if seeing Tasha like that had brought back memories of watching her mother die.

"You can go," Maddy turned to face Zane. "You've gone above and beyond, running all over the city, driving us everywhere."

"Hey, I'm no quitter, in for a penny, in for a pound," Zane said with a smile and took her hand in his. "I'm going nowhere. You never know when you might need someone to do a coffee run... or a donut one?" He hugged her and led her to a chair.

THE OVERHEAD LIGHT cast a greenish glow over the room as Ashley sat with her eyes closed, leaning on Kyle's shoulder. Maddy's head was thrown back, and Zane's coat was covering her.

The beleaguered ticking of the clock on the wall marked each painfully slow second. Zane shifted in his seat, his eyes opening long enough to notice Rick standing, staring at them. He quietly rose and went to greet him.

"Hey man," he said, his voice so low it was almost a whisper. "Glad you made it safe and sound. Have you talked to anyone?"

Rick gave him a tired half-smile and nodded. Zane patted him on the back.

"They said she's doing well and let me in to see her for a few short minutes," Rick said. "She looks so pale and helpless."

Zane feigned not noticing the quiver in Rick's voice and the wetness of his eyes.

"When the doctor stopped by here earlier, he said she was doing good," he offered, trying to encourage Rick. "Come and sit down, my friend," he said. "You must be beyond tired from your flight and the shock of all this."

Dark circles marred his usually handsome face. His shirt was rumpled and was beginning to show some dampness under the arms.

"I can't. I'm too wound up right now." Rick closed his eyes for a minute and sighed. "Do you know what happened? The doctor told me how she's doing, but he didn't know how it happened," Rick asked as he ran his hands through his hair, leaving it standing on end.

"We're not really sure," Zane said. "She was leaving the restaurant after hearing someone she thought was the killer of the chef speaking with another man. On her way to her car, she was attacked."

"She called me in Vegas. I heard some of the confrontation between Tasha and the asshole who did this to her. Do they still not know who it was? The men she overheard?"

"No, they need to talk to her first to find out exactly what she heard or saw, and which sous-chef is the one whose voice she recognized. That may lead them to the other man."

"He's a dead man walking," Rick said. "I'm going to kill him, slowly and painfully, kill him." His tone was flat. Zane saw the murderous look in his eyes and was glad it wasn't directed at him. He did not envy the person who brought that look to Rick's eyes.

"I think we all feel that way. I can only imagine what it must be like for you," Zane said.

"I have to update my mom. I'm going to call her out in the hallway."

"Alright, let me know if I can go get you a coffee or anything."

151

"Thanks, man," Rick said, looking at him and nodding. "Thanks for being here for my family," he added, gesturing toward his friends who were sitting there in various states of unconsciousness.

Maddy began to stir in her chair, looking uncomfortable. Zane was pretty sure that she was going to have a nasty kink in her neck when she awoke. The noise of her shifting caused Ashley to wake up with a start and look around, trying to orient herself.

"Any news?" she asked.

"Nothing different, only that she's resting well," Zane told her. "And Rick's arrived."

"He's here?"

"Yes, he's been to see Tasha. He's in the hallway calling his mother."

"Oh, thank God. I was so afraid something bad was going to happen while he was gone." Ashley's eyes filled with tears, and Zane realized that throughout this whole ordeal, she had remained strong and stoic. She was quite the woman. He took her hands and smiled. "She's going to be okay, Ashley."

"Is that Rick?" Maddy asked through bleary eyes. She had woken up to the sound of her friends talking. They looked down the hallway through the doorway, and all they saw was a shadow moving down the hall.

"He's out there, on the phone with his mother," Zane told her. "That was just someone walking by."

"Oh, okay," she rubbed her eyes and yawned.

"I think we should say hello to Rick and then get ourselves home," Ashley told Maddy. "We all need some rest, or else we'll end up being completely useless to Rick and Tasha. Why don't you come with me and stay in my guest room? That way, when we wake up, we can come right back here."

Rick walked into the waiting room, and both Maddy and Ashley rushed to him. They threw their arms around him and squeezed so hard that Zane was surprised the guy could still breathe.

"Okay, so which one of you decided to start investigating the murder?" Rick asked them as he pulled away.

"This time it wasn't either of us," Ashley said while making a cross over her heart. "I swear. We had asked Tasha for some names of people who worked at the restaurant, but that didn't have anything to do with her getting stabbed."

"She would probably have heard them one way or the other," Maddy added, not quite convinced that she had not played a role in tonight's tragic events.

"Uh-huh." Rick smiled wearily. "We'll talk about that later.

Right now, you need to go home and get some rest."

"We will. First, please tell us how your mom is handling things with the twins," Maddy asked.

"She is holding down the fort, as I knew she would," Rick said. "The women in my life are made of strong stuff. Including my friends." It was his turn to reach out and hug his friends. His shoulders began to heave as he buried his head. They stood there for a while, rubbing Rick's back and trying to soothe him. Zane watched as the three friends comforted each other. He could not help but feel like he was looking in from the outside, watching people who shared a special bond. He had never seen such support and love between people who were not blood relatives. He envied that about them. Not for the first time, he wondered what could have affected Maddy so badly that she had chosen friends for relatives.

Maddy took in a deep breath and exhaled. "Alright, I'm ready to go now," she said, wiping tears from her eyes. "Ashley, if that offer stands, I'd love to crash at your place."

"Absolutely."

"I can stay if you want," Zane said, turning to address Rick. "Or if you need anything, I can make a run to the 24-hour corner store?"

"That's okay, man, thanks. I think I'll take your advice from earlier and sit down to rest a bit."

"I'm going to go and see if we can get you a blanket and pillow," Ashley said and quickly took off down the hall. Now that she had something to do, she was a woman on a mission.

Maddy collected her stuff and reached over to nudge Kyle awake.

"You could sleep through an earthquake, eh?" she teased him as he stirred.

"It comes from hours of doing stakeouts in a car." Kyle raised his arms above his head and stretched. "When you finally crash, you crash hard." He looked around and sat up. "Where's Ashley?"

"I'm right here, Kyle. I went to get some things to make Rick more comfortable before we leave for the night," she said, re-entering the room.

"Good thinking, Ash." He took the pillow and blanket to give to Rick. "I'm going to stay here until the first night officer arrives, then I'll go home myself to try and catch some winks. I'll be back in the morning."

Maddy, Ashley, and Zane said their goodbyes to Rick and promised to be back in a few hours.

As they walked down the hallway past the nurse's station, Maddy reached out and gave Zane a quick side hug.

"Thank you for being here and helping out," she said.

"I didn't do much. I couldn't simply abandon you both when things were unravelling all around you."

"You were amazing and helpful, driving us around, keeping us calm and knowing when to just let me process things," Maddy replied with a tired and grateful smile.

"I agree, Zane, you were our rock," Ashley said, gratitude also evident on her face.

"If there is anything else you need, just call," he said. "I'm serious, if you need errands run or a ride somewhere, just let me know."

As they walked out of the hospital, something niggled at the back of Maddy's mind. She mentally waded through her emotions and realized something had begun to bother her while they walked down the empty hallway. The empty hallway. The shadow on the wall. A sense of dread welled up within her. Who was casting the shadow on the wall they had seen earlier, if it had not been Rick?

'Oh lord, I must be more tired than I thought,' she told herself. Simply because they had not seen anyone in the hallway when they had left, it did not mean that no one had walked by at all. It could have been any number of hospital staff, from cleaners to technicians or nurses, who were passing by. She tried to shake off the feeling as she leaned her head back in the passenger seat and closed her eyes. She was much too tired to think straight.

Chapter 20

MONDAY

Maddy had a deep and dreamless sleep. When she got up, she was surprised not to have had any nightmares. She supposed that they would come once she was rested enough to allow them to enter her subconscious mind and haunt her. Until then, she would happily go without. Having not heard anything from Rick since they had left, they decided this meant it was good news. Or at least, if anything, not bad, they reasoned.

After having one of the most refreshing showers Maddy had ever enjoyed, she came out to find her clothes clean and folded on the bed. She rapidly got dressed, and they headed out.

"Ash, did you wash and dry my clothes?" She asked as Ashley pulled her car out of the garage.

"Yes, I did."

"When did you get the chance to do that?"

"I couldn't fall asleep right away," answered Ashley. So I decided to do a load of laundry. I snuck into your room and grabbed your things. I threw them in the dryer when I woke up this morning." Ashley felt a tad responsible for Tasha's situation. She knew that, logically, it was not her fault. She had not done anything to endanger her. Tasha had to go in anyway to call the staff and patrons to let them know the restaurant would be closed until things were straightened out. Ashley was also upset over Mac's death. She and Mac had not gotten to know each other well yet or well enough to get attached to him, but Ashley had liked him a lot.

"Ashley? Where did your mind go? Did you even hear a word I said to you just now?" Maddy was watching her.

"What?"

"I said the light is green!"

"Oh, sorry. I was lost in thought."

"About last night?"

"Yes, and about Mac."

"I thought so. I was so caught up in what happened to Tasha that I didn't even stop to think how his death could have affected you. I'm so sorry, Ashley, sweetheart. I truly am."

"Thanks, hon. I'm tired of this dating game. It's starting to take its toll on me."

"I hear you."

"No, seriously. I think I need a break. Mac's death and almost losing Tasha last night, well. I need to reevaluate my life, reevaluate my priorities."

"You know what I need right now?" Maddy asked. "No, what?"

"Breakfast," she said, trying to lighten the mood. "I need to put me some Timmies in my tummy."

"Want to know something?" Ashley replied. "What?"

"Me too, girlfriend, me too."

They made a quick stop through the donut shop drive-thru next to the Royal Alexandra Hospital and picked up breakfast sandwiches for whoever might be there. They also grabbed a full breakfast, coffee, and, of course, several cookies for Rick. Chances were that he had probably neglected to eat, choosing instead to spend every moment at Tasha's bedside.

Pulling into the hospital parking lot, they saw Kyle waving at them from the front of the hospital. He was waiting at the entrance, holding the door open. He too had a tray of coffee and a box of Timbits.

"It's a Timmie's kind of morning, isn't it?" Ashley said in a faux chipper voice.

"It sure is," Kyle agreed, greeting her with a warm smile. "Are you just coming back now, or did you step out to do a coffee run?" Maddy asked as they headed toward the family waiting room on Tasha's ward.

"Just arriving," he answered. "I stopped by the station first to see if they had anything new about the case."

"And?" Ashley asked.

"They've run the plates that Tasha was able to get, and they belong to one of the sous-chefs who works at the restaurant. They are in the process of trying to track him down as he wasn't at the address on file with the Department of Motor Vehicles."

"So, what you're telling us is that he's out there, running loose?" This did not please Maddy.

"Don't worry, Tasha has 24-hour protection. No one is going to get access to her except those who are supposed to."

The family room was empty when they arrived. They spread out breakfast on the coffee table and took the cups from their cardboard trays. They were sorting through the Timbits when Rick joined them.

"Oh, this looks amazing," Rick said as he dug into the food Maddy handed him. "I didn't realize how hungry I was until the smell of that coffee wafted down the hall into Tasha's room. I hoped it was you guys."

"When did you last eat, Rick?" Ashley asked.

"Hmm... I don't quite remember. For sure, I ate something on the plane coming home. They handed out some pretzels."

"Then eat up," Maddy encouraged. "Have you heard anything from the doctors this morning?"

"Yes, and this morning I got to go sit with her on and off for thirty minutes at a time, although she hasn't regained consciousness." He took a bite of food. "Instead of the two-minute short check-ins on her, they allowed me throughout the night." He took another bite. "Oh, this is so good."

Kyle's head rose quickly from his bacon and egg bagel. "She's not awake?"

"No, she isn't. The doctor doing the rounds this morning stopped in and spoke with me," Rick told them. "She said that Tasha was very lucky, the blade barely missed her liver. Only a few millimeters over, and it would have been damaged. Thankfully, it missed all of her organs." He took a sip of coffee and sighed. "They were giving her pain control medication through an IV all through the night, and it's what's making her sleep right now."

"How long will they be giving her that medication?" Maddy asked.

"They reduced the dose when the doctor and her team came through," Rick replied. "She should become more alert as the morning progresses. They wanted to ensure that she did not feel any pain for the first few hours as she recovered from surgery." He looked at the table. "Is that a box of cookies? You guys thought of everything. I love you!" He reached for the box and took one. "Thankfully, Tasha's going to be okay. She'll just need a lot of rest to heal properly."

"That sounds very promising, Rick." Kyle smiled. "Don't forget, though, we need to talk to her as soon as she is able."

"I know, I want to catch the animal who did this to my wife as much, if not more, than the police do."

They heard a commotion in the hall, several people were approaching the family waiting room, and three distinct voices were talking excitedly. Sophia and Chloe came bursting through the door. Mama Leila came in behind them, slowly shaking her head.

"Rick, habibi, can you believe these two? I tried to convince them to stay at home. They refused to listen, threatened to order an Uber, and come over without me. Ya Allah! What could I do?" Mama Leila complained.

"Where's Mom?" Sophia asked. "We need to see her."

"Please tell us which room she's in?" Chloe asked. "You can't stop us from seeing her. She's our mother and we're worried about her!"

"I'm not even going to try to stop you," Rick replied. "Don't worry. She's resting in her room right now, though, okay?" He placed an arm around each of their shoulders. Maddy remembered when they were much smaller and he would do the same thing, back then, his hands would go on top of their heads. As their father, he had always tried to be the stabilizing force in their lives, helping them keep grounded no matter what was happening around them. That is what a good father is supposed to be, she thought as she observed them together.

Although Chloe and Sophia were twins, they were not identical. As fraternal twins, they looked like most sisters did, different with familial features. Chloe had dark, almost jet-black hair like her father's and blue-grey eyes. Sophia had Tasha's auburn hair, green eyes, and temperament. They had kept their parents hopping when they were little girls. Now, as teenagers, it was a whole other ballgame. Their drama and headaches were just beginning.

"Look, you can go to her room and check in on her. No talking, though. She won't be able to talk to you, so no disturbing her, okay? She's still pretty drugged up and out of it," he told them. "Don't get upset by the tubes and stuff she has running in and out of her either. It's scary, but the doctors say she is doing very well."

"Baba!" Chloe said, looking at her father with a long-suffering expression on her face.

"Dad, we're not children anymore," Sophia said. "We're not going to wake her up or faint at the sight of needles and such."

"I'm just preparing you." Rick then leaned over and kissed his mother on the cheek. "Thank you so much for looking after the girls, Mama."

"They're no problem at all." She kissed him back on both cheeks and hugged him tightly. "I prayed all night that God would keep our Tasha in his hands and let her come out of this in one piece. I'm going to go to church this afternoon and light some candles too."

"I love you, Mama," Rick said, hugging her back, the tension in his body melting away before he headed out into the hallway, motioning to his daughters to follow him.

"Did you two get all your homework done that was due?" Rick asked them. "You're missing school today, you have to make sure to keep up. We Nassers don't slouch off."

"Yeah, yeah," came the chorused response.

They stopped a couple of feet from Tasha's door, and Rick turned to look at them. He reached out and placed one hand on Chloe's cheek and said, "You can't be long, your mother has been through a lot and she needs to rest." As he switched his hand to Sophia's cheek, a lab tech carrying a blood testing kit passed by them and stood at the door waiting for the officer guarding it to let him through. He nodded at them as he entered the room.

"No excited chatter, keep your voices down," Rick added. Chloe took her father's hand and held it for a moment.

"We know, Baba, give us some credit," she softened her words with a small smile that her father returned.

"Okay, in you go. Don't get too close to her until the tech finishes up."

"Do you want a coffee or anything, Officer Haru?" he asked the police officer who had sat back down in the chair placed for him next to Tasha's door. "We have lots."

"Sure, that would be gre..."

A loud clanging noise came from Tasha's room, and the two men looked at each other in alarm. Loud grunting and yelling could be heard. Before either man could react and open the door, the room became eerily silent, followed by a man's voice swearing that he'd murder someone. Rick and the officer flung open the door and stared in disbelief at the scene before them. Chloe and Sophia had the lab technician sprawled on the floor. Sophia was sitting on his back, holding one of his arms behind him, twisted at an alarming angle.

Chloe was sitting on his legs, tying them up tightly with a tourniquet rubber band, a murderous look on her face. He was squirming and trying to buck the two girls off him, unable to get enough momentum with only one free limb.

"It's over there". Chloe motioned frantically with her head, pointing to what appeared to be an over-bed table lying on its side.

Rick ran to see what she was pointing at. Sophia got off the man's back while Officer Haru took out his handcuffs and fastened them to the man's wrists. Chloe got out of his way and stood beside her sister, who was watching with interest. Rick joined them. He was holding a knife by its tip and as far away from his body as possible.

"These girls are loons! You need to arrest them," the lab tech impersonator cried out. "One of them kicked my arm and broke it! And get this rubber band off of me, I can't feel my legs."

"What's going on here? Why did you wrestle the lab tech to the ground?" Officer Haru asked.

"He was going to kill Mom!" exclaimed Sophia.

"We had no choice," Chloe added.

"We caught him..."

"He was standing over Mom..."

"He had that knife..."

"Sir, is this your knife?" asked Officer Haru, pointing at the weapon in Rick's hand.

"Yes. I need it to cut... lab stuff," the lab tech replied. "You know, rubber bands, cotton wads, needles."

"You need a large kitchen knife to cut needles, do you?" asked Officer Haru, checking to make sure the handcuffs were secure.

"I was so scared, Baba!" Chloe said, hugging her father.

"Chloe was amazing..." Sophia said.

"Thanks, you too, sis!"

"We sure showed him..." Chloe added with a smirk.

"Those Cobra Kai kids have nothing on us!" Sophia said, fist-bumping her sister.

"I told you those girls are certifiable!" the wannabe lab tech yelled as the officer tried to pull him up to his feet, rubber band still tied around his legs.

"I highly recommend you hold your peace or you might accidentally trip and hurt yourself," Rick shouted at him.

"Can't an injured woman get any peace and quiet around here?" Tasha asked.

Chapter 21

Peple drawn by all the commotion had gathered in the hallway outside Tasha's hospital room. Kyle noticed all the people and went to investigate. Once he realized it was Tasha's room they were gathered around, he told Maddy and Ashley to stay with Rick's mom. He made his way down the hall and tried to push his way through without much success. Finally, he had had enough of people refusing to let him get by.

"Police, let me through!" He bellowed with authority, holding his detective's badge high over his head. Once in the room, his eyes went wide. Taking in the bizarre scene before him, all he could think of was 'Why is it always my friends? Why can't it be the neighbor down the street? This is on Officer Haru's watch, not mine. I swear, if it wasn't for Ashley...' His thoughts were rambling on in his head until Rick interrupted them.

"Kyle! Do something! That... that... jerk tried to kill Tasha," he spat out between clenched teeth, watching Kyle just standing there, staring at them.

"Detective O'Grady, can you please secure the scene as best as you can while I take care of the suspect?" Officer Haru asked.

"Of course." Now he was being drawn into it professionally. He wished that, for once, his name would not be attached to any criminal situation where Maddy or her friends were involved. This was the third time in recent memory. "Have you called it in?"

"Yes, they're sending a team now. Could you also please find a bag and take the knife from the husband?" He pointed at the weapon Rick was still holding by the tip of his fingers. "He's done a good job of keeping his fingerprints off it, but he looks like he might drop it at any time... or use it."

Kyle found a bag for the disposal of hazardous waste on the wall near the washroom. He put on a pair of blue examination gloves and took the knife from Rick.

"Hey, Rick, looks like this is going to be all over soon. Take a deep breath, hug your wife and girls. Everyone's okay."

"Thanks, Kyle," Rick said.

"I'll take a pic of this jerk before they take him away. I want to see if Tasha recognizes him when she's a little more coherent," Kyle said.

"Okay, good. I suspect his prints will match the ones on the knife we have in evidence."

KYLE SENT EVERYONE away while he secured Tasha's room, which now doubled as a crime scene. The detectives who were looking after this case had wanted to move her out of it. The nurses would have none of it and put their foot down, saying they did not have another room available. That did not go over well with the detectives. In the end, they agreed to do some quick work while Tasha was being taken to get some X-rays done on the arm she had landed on when she had been pushed to the ground before getting stabbed.

When Rick and the girls returned to the family room, they found Maddy and Ashley anxiously waiting for them. They had many questions on their minds as they had seen Officer Haru walk someone by in handcuffs.

"What on earth happened, girls?" Maddy asked.

"My incredibly brave daughters decided to tackle a man twice their size and throw him to the floor. Doing everything, including hog-tying him," Rick said, a hint of pride tinging his voice.

"That's pretty much it," said Sophia.

"Yup, pretty much," confirmed Chloe.

The room broke out in a babble of questions.

"Who was it?"

Are you okay?"

"Where is he now?"

It took Rick a few minutes before he was able to calm everyone down and answer their questions as best as he could. When he was done, everyone turned to look at the twins in amazement until, finally, Maddy spoke up.

"That's super cool, young ladies!" Maddy high-fived them.

"You guys have to be careful," Ashley told them, shaking her head and rubbing her forehead, feeling a tension migraine coming on. "Using martial arts is considered a weapon. But I won't tell if you don't."

The twins stood there with grins spread across their faces. They were enjoying the attention and feeling quite good about themselves until they saw their grandmother sitting in the corner, crossing herself over and over while holding a rosary and repeating prayers. She stopped long enough to give them a look that warned them of the lecture that was to come once she was done. There was nothing more dreadfully frightening than an angry Middle Eastern grandmother.

A female officer came into the waiting room, accompanied by a social worker, to ask if they could interview the girls and take their statements in a side room. Rick could be present if he liked. All three looked at Mama Leila and decided that it would be in everyone's best interest to take advantage of this request and make their exit before her prayers were over.

An hour passed before they returned. Thankfully, Mama Leila was gone.

"Where's Teta Leila?" asked Chloe.

"I sent her home in an Uber," Ashley replied. "She looked exhausted. I told her one of us would drive you home when you were ready to leave."

"Thank you, that was very thoughtful of you," Rick said, relief all over his face. A ding brought his attention to his cell phone. "Hey, the picture I asked Kyle to send me just came through." Kyle had sent several pictures of the suspect. Rick hurried out of the room, saying over his shoulder, "I have to show Tasha the pictures of this guy and then text Kyle back. I'll return as soon as I'm done."

WHEN RICK ENTERED TASHA'S hospital room, he saw her lying in her bed with her eyes closed, resting. He nodded to Officer Haru, who was sitting in a chair against the far wall, apparently waiting for Tasha to wake up. Rick quietly approached the bed. As he looked down at Tasha, a warm feeling spread throughout him. This woman meant everything to him. The mother of his children, his soulmate, his fiery Italian habibti. He wiped a tear that had escaped and thought about how close he had come to a life without her.

"Enough of your blubbering, don't you have the girl's homework to check?" his wife murmured.

"It can wait," he said with a smile. "Right now, nothing is going to stop me from staring at my beautiful wife."

"I'm going to step outside for a minute," Kyle said to no one in particular. Neither of the Nassers acknowledged his departure.

"Just don't come too close, Rick, my mouth feels like something that ate 10 bowls of your mama's garlic toom just died in it."

"Yeah... I was going to mention that to you." He laughed.

She tried to playfully smack him, but it ended up being more of a weak wave in his direction with her left hand because her dominant arm was bandaged up.

"I'm sorry, I know you must be exhausted, but I need you to look at a picture for me, please."

"What's it a picture of?"

"I was hoping you could tell me who this is." He brought his phone up and turned it around so she could see the photos Kyle had texted him.

"Oh, I know him," Tasha looked like she was searching her memory for a name. "He was in the restaurant to talk to Chef Mackenzie, he's some other chef."

"He's not one of the sous-chefs?"

"No, he's not. Our sous-chefs are Dimitri, Jayda, and Sebastian," Tasha replied.

"Do you know anything else about him, like why he might want Mackenzie dead?"

"I don't know why he would, but his name is 'François'. He's supposed to be French," she said, her voice getting quieter by the minute.

"Supposed to be French?"

"Yeah, but his accent was horrible. It wasn't a real French accent," Tasha said. "I thought at the time he was just being pretentious."

"Okay, you rest now, sweetheart. You need to get well enough for us to take you home. My mom is just itching to do some cooking and serve you in bed."

Tasha moaned quietly and smiled. "Mio Dio! She'll have a captive audience in me. I'm going to end up stuffed like a cannoli!"

"It'll give you incentive to get back on your feet." Rick kissed her forehead, gently tucked the blanket around her, and left her to rest some more. Somehow, she had managed to sleep through most of the morning's commotion. Those had been some powerful drugs going through her IV.

Outside the hospital room, Kyle was standing, talking on his phone. He raised a single finger, indicating he wanted Rick to hang around for a minute. While he waited for Kyle to be done, Rick looked through the door's window and stared at his sleeping wife. She looked so small, pale, and vulnerable laying there; her arm was all bandaged up, an iv was going through her arm, some kind of monitor was attached to her chest, a blood oxygen monitor was on one finger, and a blood pressure cuff had been wrapped around her good arm, going off every hour. It made his heart ache. Anger rose within him. Someone had to pay, and someone would, somehow.

"That was the station," Kyle said as he put his phone away. "Lots happening, they didn't even have to locate the sous-chef. His name's Dimitri Vasiliou. When he found out Tasha was attacked and that afterwards someone had tried to kill her here at the hospital, he started singing like the proverbial canary."

"What'd he say?"

"Well, he denies knowing anything about Mackenzie Davis's murder. He said he was talking to a chef by the name of..." Kyle paused to take a look at a note on his phone. "Here it is, 'François'. He said that he had previously told Chef François that he was upset with Davis over some scheduling issue. He made the mistake of saying he could kill him. He said the guy took him seriously and took care of Davis for him."

"Do you believe him?" Rick asked.

"We're going to wait and see what this 'François' fellow has to say, and we need to check out Dimitri's alibi. He says he was at an Oilers game when Davis was killed. That should be fairly easy to check out."

"What about Tasha?"

"All he said was that shortly after they left the restaurant, François called him on his cell to tell him someone had come out after them, but not to worry, he'd take care of it. Then he hung up." Kyle relayed their conversation to him. "He said the guy was certifiably crazy, and that's why he confessed everything he knew. He didn't want any more deaths on his conscience, or anything that could lead to his own untimely demise."

Chapter 22

"It's been a while since I've been to Iconoclast," Maddy said. "Good choice for a coffee spot, Zane."

"I thought you might need a distraction after all the events of the last couple of weeks."

"Yeah, thanks, it's been quite a month, that's for sure." She took three packages of turbinado sugar for her coffee and a spoon to stir with to their table. "Add to it that we missed saying goodbye to our little Ryan."

"That was certainly a big disappointment. But the people at the sanctuary strongly believe that he might come back around there to mate and nest next Spring," Zane said, hoping that sharing this information might cheer her up. "We can always drive around and maybe find him when the Canada Geese come back to Edmonton."

"I guess we could do that. It might be fun."

"Yes! Like our scavenger hunt was. We enjoyed that, even if we didn't win a year's supply of Pietro's pizza."

"Yeah, that part was a real bummer." Maddy laughed, remembering how she had almost begged the pizza place's owner for some free pizza. It was another of her not-so-proud moments.

"Hey guys, glad I found you here," Kyle said as he approached their table, dragging a chair over and taking a seat.

"How did you even know we would be at this café?" Zane asked, nose a bit out of joint at having his coffee time with Maddy interrupted by their friendly neighborhood detective.

"Oh, it was quite easy, I called Ashley and she told me Maddy was meeting you here this afternoon." He gave him a sardonic smile. "And look at that, here you are."

"Mmhmm, and here we are." Zane crumpled his napkin. Changing his mind, he then smoothed and folded it neatly before sliding it under his coffee cup.

"Didn't even need to be a detective to find us, eh?" kidded Maddy, elbowing him in the ribs and snorting at her joke.

"Cute," Kyle grinned. "I've been wanting to talk to you in person about the case, but didn't want to drag you into the station."

"Do you have any updates on that François guy? Did he act alone, or was that sous-chef involved more than he led on?" No matter how Zane felt about Kyle's presence at the café, he couldn't hold back his curiosity about the ongoing murder investigation.

"François, or should I say Frank Dobbs, that's his real name by the way." Kyle started to share the latest information. "He..."

"He's not French?" Maddy interrupted.

"Nope, not one bit." Kyle laughed. "Anyway, he said that a guy by the name of Damon Archer was egging him on. Something about removing the competition standing in their way for the auctioning of the knives."

"I had a feeling that Archer guy was in on it. He gave me the creeps." Maddy could always read people pretty well.

"The detectives are trying to locate him to bring him in for questioning," Kyle told them. "I haven't been told much else."

"Hopefully, he hasn't skipped town." Zane didn't look very impressed that they had not found Damon Archer yet.

"We'll find him," Kyle told Maddy. "They did say that if they couldn't find him today that they would put a warrant out for him as a person of interest. He shouldn't get too far."

"If he's not gone already," Zane said under his breath. Kyle heard him and gave him a disapproving look.

"Thanks for sharing what you do know. We appreciate everything the Edmonton Police Services are doing," Maddy said, trying to smooth things over after Zane's remarks. She wondered where on earth that attitude of his was coming from. "Now, tell me what's up?" Maddy straightened her back against her chair, fearing what might come next. "You sought me out for a reason, right?"

"Do you want me to leave you two alone?" asked Zane.

"No, that's alright. It's nothing sensitive or anything like that," Kyle said.

"Just tear the Band-Aid off, Kyle, don't make me wait." Maddy was not the patient sort these days.

"We're going to have to keep the whole knife roll and all the knives as evidence until the case goes to court."

"What? No!" Maddy's dream shop evaporated right in front of her eyes. "But they're worth a lot of money. I need it to open my store."

"Maddy, you'll get them back," Zane said. "Once the case is over, they'll return them to you, maybe even sooner if the police and prosecutor don't need them, right, Kyle?"

Kyle looked at Zane, impressed by his knowledge. "Yeah, that's correct. The detectives on the case have taken all the pictures they needed and have already filed their report. The case is on the prosecutor's desk. She'll look at all the evidence and decide what she needs to keep."

"Rick and his daughters will probably be called in as eyewitnesses in the case of the attempted murder of Tasha," Zane added. "I'm going to presume that Tasha identifying Chef François in the photo lineup, the sous-chef 's testimony, and the prints on the knife used to kill

Chef Mackenzie will be more than enough to convict the man, without having to have your knives present."

"That's right," confirmed Kyle, becoming more and more curious about how Zane was so knowledgeable. "Most of the time, pictures of the weapon should be enough. Like Zane said, it will depend on the prosecutor."

"How long will it take?" Maddy asked, not really reassured by what they both had said to her.

"It will depend on how many cases are on the prosecutor's desk," Zane replied.

Maddy turned toward Zane and was also wondering how he knew all this stuff. "May I ask you a personal question, Zane?"

"I guess?" He hesitated in his reply. "How personal is personal?"

"Well, more nosy than personal."

"Okay, shoot."

"How come you know so much about the law?"

"Yeah, that's been on my mind too," added Kyle. The two of them stared at Zane.

"What?" Zane was taken aback by Maddy's question and Kyle's reaction. "I thought you knew, I'm studying law."

"You are? Why didn't you ever mention it before?" asked Maddy.

"Why d'you think I've been lugging around a backpack full of law books everywhere I go? Did you not see them in the back seat of my car?"

"Umm, I, umm..." Maddy felt embarrassed for not having put two and two together. "I figured you were just nerdy and liked reading those kinds of books. Kinda like me watching Criminal Minds and such."

"It all makes total sense now," mused Kyle.

"What does?" Zane asked with interest.

"All your comments about what's legal and what's not. What Ashley should and shouldn't have done," Kyle remarked. "You weren't being pushy, you were doing what comes naturally."

"Pardon me?" Zane was not sure if he had been insulted or complimented. Either way, he was slightly taken aback by Kyle's comment.

"Don't get me wrong. That's all cool, now that I know where you were coming from."

Maddy listened and watched them both circling each other, feeling out if they could be friends, frenemies, or find a peaceful accord. She would never understand the male ego. When she thought the two guys had reached an acceptable standstill, she interrupted them.

"Is there any way of finding out when the prosecutor might get to that file?"

"Not really, sorry Maddy." Kyle started fiddling with the sugar container. "I don't imagine it will take long, not a murder case."

"Do you happen to know who the prosecutor is?" Zane asked Kyle.

He stopped fiddling and looked up quizzically. "I believe it's Alexandria Jakobson. Why?"

"Excellent! I have a friend who, as it happens, is articling in her office. I'll have a chat with him and see if I can pull in a favor."

"Zane, if you could do that for me, I'd love you forever!" She smiled at him. Her spikey-haired tattooed friend, she thought, was certainly full of surprises today.

SURPRISES WERE NOT over for Maddy that day. During dinner at PopPop's, he broached the subject of his relationship with Shirley. What he shared was not at all what she had expected to hear from her grandfather. She thought, by his happy mood, that perhaps Shirley had finally made a decision and picked him over Bob. On the contrary, Maddy was mistaken, quite mistaken.

"What do you mean by 'arrangement'?" Maddy asked, confused by what PopPop meant. She just wanted to make sure that he or Shirley had told Bob what was going on behind his back. Now he was talking about them having come to some kind of arrangement.

"The three of us sat down and had a discussion like the adults we are," PopPop began. "When Bob and I agreed that Shirley had to make a decision and choose one of us, she had another suggestion."

"What was it?" Maddy had a feeling she was going to regret askings.

"I know you don't like to talk about such things with me, hon, but please hear me out, okay? The three of us have reached a certain age, when, you know, things don't always, how can I put it? Especially Bob and I..."

"Shirley is the same age as you two," Maddy pointed out.

PopPop looked at her in frustration. "This is hard enough as it is, Maddy, please let me finish without interruption."

She made a motion of zipping her lips and throwing away the key.

"Yes, Shirley is around the same age as us. Umm, things are... different for men." PopPop suddenly had trouble meeting her eyes. "And sometimes we are more interested in companionship than she is."

"Oh no," Maddy thought. 'Oh no, oh no, oh no, make it stop!'

"We both adore Shirley, yet each of us can only keep such a vibrant woman happy some of the time. If I work on making her happy part of the time, and Bob the other part of the time..."

"What. Are you. Trying to say?"

"Alright, here we go..." He took a minute to gather his thoughts and find the right way to explain their arrangement to her. "We three have agreed to what you young ones call a "

relationship."

"A what?" Maddy's jaw dropped.

"A p relationship, you know, when there's more than one romantic and intimate partner at the same time and everyone knows about it and is okay with it."

"I know what polyamorous means, PopPop!"

"Then why did you ask?"

"It wasn't a 'question' question, it was a question formulated by surprise." She could not believe what she was hearing.

"You mean a rhetorical question?" PopPop asked.

"Yes, however you want to describe it." Maddy didn't care what word he wanted to call it, she just knew she had never been more shocked in her life.

"We're all friends, sometimes we'll even go out for dinner together. We will decide beforehand which one of us will be taking her home, that's all." PopPop explained. "So, you see, you've nothing to worry about, your business relationship with Bob is safe."

"And you're okay with that?"

"Yes, that's why it's a polyamo..."

"Don't, it's not necessary to repeat yourself."

'What are old people coming to these days?' Maddy thought. 'Whatever happened to baking cookies and doing the daily crossword puzzle?'

Chapter 23

THURSDAY

"Hey, Ashley! Am I ever happy to see you!" Joshua pulled a chair closer to her desk and sat down. "I tried to catch you before you left for the day yesterday. I must have just missed you."

"Hello Josh," she greeted him with a smile. She always enjoyed when her dapper colleague dropped by her office for a visit. She had not seen Joshua since he had priced out Maddy's knives. "Yes, I had a meeting in Spruce Grove with a potential client. He wants to turn a barn into some kind of fancy B&B and wants an authentic saloon bar and furniture. Not sure it's my taste, but it's not my place to question it. I'm only paid to find what my clients want."

"That's not going to be an easy task."

"Nope, most of this kind of antique isn't in the best of shape here in Alberta. I might have to venture into the United States for that, but it's not impossible." She smiled and added, "For the right price, anything is possible. Anyway, what can I do for you, good sir?"

"Did your friend Maddy get her set of knives back yet?"

"Not yet why?"

"Because they're now in much higher demand!" He opened up his laptop and showed her his email inbox screen. Then he pulled up his Reddit app. "Look at all the comments!" He scrolled to show her. "They're reaching out to me because they know that I'm the company's knife specialist. It's insane! There's nothing like getting media attention to boost the interest in an item. All those emails I showed you? People who are interested in buying the knife set. They all want to know when we will be reopening the bidding on the auction."

"This is so morbid." Ashley opened the link to the auction site. There were several messages from the site's owners, asking the same thing as the people who had emailed Joshua. "Any item attached to some sensational crime becomes a 'must-have' object. Especially if traditional mainstream media covers it, not only bloggers and social media influencers." She opened up her emails and saw thirty new ones with the title 'KNIVES'. "I haven't had the chance to check my inbox. It looks like emails about the set started coming in yesterday afternoon!"

"So, when are we reopening the auction on them, then?"

"Once Maddy gets them back from the police, I presume. IF she still wants to continue with the auction."

"Why wouldn't she?"

"It is pretty macabre, don't you think?"

"Yes, but that's what sells!"

Ashley inhaled deeply. "I suppose you're right. I'll talk to her and see if she still wants to. They would bring in a lot more than we originally thought, that's a certainty."

"Ashley?" Allyssa was knocking on the door frame to her office.

"Yes?"

"That Archer man? He's at the reception. He's demanding to see you. What should I do?" Ashley and Joshua looked at each other.

"Do you want me to stay?" he asked.

"I think it would be best if you leave," Ashley said. "He strikes me as the kind of guy who may escalate if there is a man here. He may feel he has to act macho around you."

Allyssa watched him leave, then turned back, waiting for an answer. She noticed that Ashley was staring out the window.

"Ashley?"

"Bring him into my office and close the door behind you. Call security and tell them to be ready to come up. We might have a situation on our hands."

"Are you sure about that? It doesn't seem like a safe thing to do."

"Yes, I'm certain. Please, bring him in."

Ashley grabbed a heavy paperweight from the far end of her desk and brought it nearer to her. She closed her eyes and calmed herself down. Archer didn't need to know that she was nervous.

"Mister Archer, what brings you here on this lovely Thursday morning?" she asked as Allyssa led him in and closed the door as instructed.

"I heard that the auction has been paused and that the few people who were interested in taking part in bidding on my knives are no longer going to be for various, ahem, reasons," he snidely remarked.

"Alright, and why would it change anything concerning you?" Ashley needed to stretch their conversation. "Ms. Whitman is still their owner, not you."

"Let's not allow minor details to distract us from the point that they are now available for me to buy since they're not being auctioned off." He grinned and sat down.

"Well, they're not available, not at the moment anyway. It's my understanding that the police have yet to release them." She grinned back. "One of them was used as a murder weapon, after all. The others are also being kept as evidence."

"Here you go with minor details again. Once they are returned to her, she can sell them to me." He started to show some frustration and was having difficulty trying to control his temper.

"I can ask Ms. Whitman if she would sell them to you." Ashley's mind was racing, trying to make up a story to keep him in her office and execute the plan she had in mind. "You are aware that they are now worth at least double their original price?"

"What?" He stood up and leaned over her desk. "You cannot be serious? Nobody in their right mind would pay that!"

"One would tend to think as you do, and yet I have here many emails from people who you might describe as not being 'in their right mind' offering huge sums of money for them."

Devon Archer slammed his fist down. "I've had enough of this! You get this Maddy Whitman woman on the phone this instant and make her sell me these knives at a reasonable price, or else YOU will be paying the price."

"Okay, take it easy, I'll make a call to her office." She picked up her phone and dialed a number. "I'll let her know how strongly you feel about it."

"Maddy? I have Mr. Damon Archer in my office right now. Yes, the owner of the locker you purchased. The one that had the knives in it," she said. "He really, really wants to buy them. He's quite upset and is being very insistent. No, I don't think that he'll take no for an answer. You will? You will sell them to him? Okay. I'll let him know." She hung up the phone and looked up at him. He did not look as pleased as she thought he would.

"She said you could have them and can pay monthly if you wish. I'll draw up the papers, if you could please sit down."

"Do you take me for a fool? You didn't call her. Nobody was on the other end of the line." He roared in anger. "You pick up that damn phone right now and call the bitch. I want you to put that conversation on speaker phone, do you understand me?"

"I think you need to calm down or this conversation will be over this instant!" Ashley was starting to shake.

"I'll tell you what will be over this instant, you idiotic woman!" he growled as he came around her desk.

Ashley stood up, her hand resting on the paperweight.

"Let me give you a taste of what's in store for you if you don't call her immediately." He shoved her backwards, and she stumbled over her chair, dropping the paperweight in the process. They both watched it roll on the floor, out of her reach.

"You thought you could use that on me? Maybe I should use it on you?" He loomed over her.

The door swung open, and a security guard stepped in.

"Move away from her this minute," he ordered.

"Or what?" Archer snarled. "You'll grab me by the collar and try to drag me out?"

"No, we'll shoot you in the shoulder, perhaps we'll miss, perhaps we won't," a determined voice said over the guard's shoulder as two police officers walked in behind, guns drawn.

"Oh, thank God!" Ashley whispered. Taking advantage of Archer being distracted, she crawled as far away from him as her office space would allow and stood up.

"I don't know how or when, but I will get you for this!" he yelled at Ashley as one of the officers was putting handcuffs on him and the other read him his rights.

Joshua and Allyssa stepped into her office. Allyssa hugged her and then righted the chair, telling her to sit down.

"I can't sit, I'm too pumped up on adrenaline." She then gestured toward the two officers. "How did the police get here so fast?" she asked. "I just called Kyle."

"Joshua called them as soon as he left your office," Allyssa said.

"I knew he was the knives' previous owner," Joshua explained. "I also knew his reputation went further than drinking and gambling. He's had a few run-ins with the law for brawling, so..."

Ashley spontaneously gave him a big hug. "I can't thank you enough!"

"Are you alright, Ashley? I came as fast as I could," Kyle flashed his badge as he walked into the room.

"Oh, Kyle!" Ashley ran into his arms and started to cry.

"Hey, hey, it's okay," he whispered, kissing her on the head. "Your colleague here is one smart guy. I'd put in a good word for him at his next evaluation." This made her smile. "After you phoned me and started talking like I was Maddy, I knew something was off. I called it in and was told that a car was already there. I ran right over."

"The benefits of your station being nearby," Ashley said. "Please, never transfer, okay?"

"I promise."

Chapter 24

SUNDAY

"Girls, keep it down!" Rick implored. "Your mother's supposed to be resting, please take your arguments elsewhere!"

"But Dad," complained Sophia. "Chloe refuses to give me the answer to this math equation!"

"That's what you're arguing about? There will be no cheating in this house. Take your homework to your rooms and get out of here." Sophia started to protest. "NOW!" he bellowed, losing his patience.

Stretching out on the couch, a stack of pillows behind her back, Tasha rolled her eyes. Her biggest distraction to her restful healing was Rick himself. He barely gave her a minute alone. He constantly hovered around her, asking if she wanted something to drink, if she was comfortable, or if she needed another pillow. To say he doted on her would be putting it mildly.

"Let them be Rick, they're just being teenagers," she said. "This isn't a funeral home, believe me, I'm familiar with what they are like."

Rick grumbled under his breath, and she smiled to herself. She had to admit she found his attention endearing.

"Tasha, habibti, I made some hummus. I'll bring a bowl with some pita." Mama Leila came into the living room, wearing an apron with 'Born to Shop, Forced to Cook' printed on it and a wooden spoon in hand.

Speaking of attention, Tasha thought, 'I will be the only woman who was stabbed, underwent surgery, and came out of it having gained weight.'

The doorbell rang, and Rick went to answer it. There was a cacophony of voices at the front door, which quickly settled down to barely discernible whispers. She did manage to recognize the three voices conversing in their foyer.

"Ignore Rick, you guys, I don't need silence," she called out to her friends. "It was my stomach that was stabbed, not my brain."

They entered the room in a flurry of balloons, brightly colored parcels, and a fruit tray.

"Tasha!" Maddy said. "You look fabulous! You're the only woman I know who can get stabbed and still look gorgeous."

"Doesn't she?" Ashley chimed in. "She has some healthy color in her cheeks, too!"

"She must be eating some good home cooking," Zane said, looking at the large bowl of hummus surrounded by pita chips.

"Umm... I'm right here, guys," Tasha said. "I can hear you and everything."

"Of course you can, hon." Maddy patted her knee like she was a doddering old lady who needed to be placated.

"Where should we put these balloons?" Ashley asked, looking at Rick.

"You could tie them on the back of that chair or the stair railing?" Tasha answered instead.

"And the fruit?" Maddy asked.

"I can take it into the kitchen." Rick reached for the tray.

"Don't you dare take it away from me, I need some fruit!" Tasha said. "Home cooking is all well and good, but this lady needs some fiber."

The friends took off their rain jackets, and after some shuffling around, they managed to organize themselves on the living room armchairs.

"Is there any news on the case?" Tasha asked, feeling so disconnected from what was happening outside her home's four walls. While being wrapped in a cocoon of family love was something she was blessed to have, she was beginning to get restless.

"François has confessed to everything. I mean, they got him literally with the weapon in his hot little hands. His fingerprints were also on the quail knife, and he has no alibi for when Mackenzie was killed," Zane said.

"But why?" Tasha asked. "I only saw him at the restaurant a couple of times. He seemed to be on pretty good terms with Chef Mackenzie. Why would he kill him?"

"Well, let's just say that François had personal reasons that we may not understand," Maddy said. "His real name is Frank Dobbs. He is convinced that he's the reincarnation of the original owner of the knife set. We have no idea what's with that, things are a bit fuzzy around where that weirdness comes in. He wanted them back, and Chef Mackenzie was standing in his way."

"How was he doing that?" Tasha tried to sit up but quickly changed her mind when the pain reminded her of her recent surgery.

"He knew Chef Mackenzie was interested in bidding on the knives because, believe it or not, Damon Archer told him about them."

"Isn't he the lunatic owner of the locker you found the knives in?" Tasha asked.

"Yup." Maddy nodded.

"That's not all." Ashley picked up the story where Maddy left off. "Damon Archer knew that Chef François was loonie toons. He taunted him about the knives, hoping that he would go after Mackenzie and convince him not to participate in the auction. Maybe even remove François from the bidding, too, if he, in turn, did something illegal and got arrested. Archer knew that François would stop at nothing to get those knives, even if it involved taking poor Mackenzie out of the equation. His plan worked, too well, actually. In François's mind, that clearly meant Mackenzie had to go. But how to do it? He intentionally befriended and manipulated one of the sous-chefs with a promise of a chef 's position in his new restaurant. Of course, that was mere fabrication."

"He didn't even have to try that hard," Maddy jumped in. "The sous-chef found out from Chef Mackenzie that Ashley was bringing the knives with her to the restaurant. The whole kitchen was excited about seeing them, as you well know. François asked the sous-chef to distract the staff while Chef Mackenzie was in the kitchen with Ash."

"He was digging through my carryall that I had left on the table," Ashley explained. "François had the quail knife in his hands, admiring it, when he and the sous-chef heard me getting ready to leave. The sous-chef panicked, grabbed the knife roll and bag, and then ran into the storage room. My bag wasn't where I had left it on the table, so when I walked by, I didn't see it and completely forgot all about it. I had been distracted by Mac's food and whatnot." She blushed a bit, embarrassed. "Nobody had noticed François because he had hidden in the coat closet. He was able to sneak out the back, unseen, a bit later. The sous-chef brought my now tidied up carryall to Mac - minus the quail knife - who then came after me with it."

"WOW!" Tasha couldn't believe that all this happened right under her nose while she was in the back office. "So, when sous-chef Dimitri was angry at Mac and made an offhand comment about wanting him dead, François ... I mean Frank, decided to kill him."

"Yes," Zane said. "It was the excuse he'd been looking for. The idea was planted in his head by Archer. He told François/ Frank to use the quail knife and leave it in Mackenzie's body so all the knives would be back together after the autopsy. He also told him to blame sous-chef

Dimitri if anyone caught him. François was loopy enough not to realize that none of that was logical."

"But did either of them think they could fly around the world killing every potential participant in the auction?" Tasha said. "That makes no sense."

"Hey, we didn't say any of it made sense. I mean, when is it a sensible thing to attack and kill a man in his own kitchen?" Zane said.

"Touché," said Tasha.

"How did you guys find out the whole story?" Rick asked. "I mean, that's a lot of details. The three guys couldn't have admitted to it, or did they?"

"It's a funny story, actually," Ashley said. "Each guy tattled on the other. Putting the blame elsewhere. The thing Archer didn't consider was that he'd spoken to Maddy and me, so we had bits of information that helped piece some of the story together. The sous-chef 's lawyer negotiated an immunity deal. Since he didn't have anything to do with the murder or attempted murder, the deal went ahead. It didn't take much to put the whole story together."

Mama Leila walked into the living room holding a serving tray that was overflowing with baked goods and a pitcher of lemonade with glasses.

"Oh my, Mama Leila," Maddy said. "You didn't have to do all that for us!"

"No problem at all, my dear," she said. "Rick, sweetheart, would you please go to the kitchen and bring the tray of baklava and cookies that's on the counter? It's heavy, and I have to get the plates and napkins."

Zane wasn't used to Mama Leila's Middle Eastern way of showing love and affection. His eyes widened at the spread that was set before him, and the knowledge that more was to come.

Tasha made eye contact with Maddy and sighed deeply as though to say, 'Look what I have to put up with.'

"Hey Maddy, I have some good news for you." Zane had a wide, goofy smile on his face. "I just received one helluva text."

"Zane, you look like the cat who ate the canary. Tell me!"

"My friend who works for the prosecutor handling the case..."

"Yes?"

"He asked her to take a quick look at it and see if they needed to have the knives present or if the pictures were enough. He explained your monetary situation and what not."

"What monetary situation?" asked Rick.

"There isn't one. I made it sound like Maddy desperately needed the money or her business would go belly up."

"Counsellor! That's perjury or something like that, isn't it?" Ashley exclaimed.

"Not quite," Zane smiled again. "One, we weren't in court. Two, I didn't lie to a judge, and three, I was never under oath. Oh, and I'm not a lawyer yet, so no harm done."

"ZANE!!! Stop chatting and tell me what the prosecutor said?" Maddy had lost all her patience and was well on the way to losing her mind, too. "Did she make a decision or not? How long will I have to wait?"

"Which question would you like me to answer first?"

"ZANE!!!" They all yelled at the same time, startling poor Mama Leila, who had re-entered the living room, making her drop all the napkins.

"You should be able to get them back in six months or so." He reached over and picked up the napkins Mama Leila had dropped. "Once they've been properly processed and all the paperwork has been filled out. That's not too bad considering it could have taken a year or two with all the backlog in the system," he said.

"Oh my God! Thank you! Thank you, Zane!" Maddy said. "I owe you big time!"

"That's twice now... I'll have to cash those IOU's soon or you might forget about them." He laughed. "Here you go, Mrs. Nasser."

"Please, call me Mama Leila. What a nice young man you brought over, girls," she remarked to Ashley and Maddy, taking the napkins from Zane. She then poured some lemonade into the glasses and passed the tray around.

"Mama Leila, you need something to keep you busy," Maddy observed as she reached for a spinach pie. "You're spending so much time baking and cooking. You're making enough food to feed two or three times the size of your family."

"I know, Tasha has been encouraging me to find a hobby or something to do," she said. "I think I may have found something, although it might take a bit to work out."

"Mama? You never mentioned this to me before!" Rick said. "What is it?"

"You've had your hands and mind occupied elsewhere, I didn't want to distract you, habibi."

"Please, Mama, distract him!" Tasha said, a twinkle in her eyes.

"A friend of mine told me about some seniors who are starting up a new catering business that is specifically aimed at other seniors." Mama went on to explain. "This group of partners requires someone who's not only good in the kitchen but also smart and dependable. It's going to be more than only catering, they want it to be like a different kind of dispensary or pharmacy, if you like."

Maddy's ears perked up at the word 'dispensary'. "What would you be doing, Mama?" Rick asked.

"They need someone to do some baking for them, so I figured, why not? I'm baking anyway."

"Is it a restaurant?"

"Oh no, habibi, that would be too much work. It's a store that's going to be specifically aimed at seniors and their... how did my friend put it? Oh, yes, it will be aimed and adapted to their natural needs. It will also have a bakery in the back where they have things specifically prepared for seniors," Mama said. " They want me to adapt some pastry recipes to include added medicinal ingredients, which will be measured correctly by certified personnel. That won't be my responsibility. I would have to make sure that they don't affect the flavor of the products."

"Oh, kind of like bran cereal or oatmeal mixed in cookies?" Tasha asked.

"Yes, something like that, sweetheart." Mama smiled and walked back to the kitchen.

Maddy felt an overwhelming sense of foreboding. Seniors, plus dispensary, plus baking... that could only mean one thing, she thought, 'Rick is going to kill me.'

Chapter 25

"I'm so full I could just burst!" Ashley said as she pulled up to Maddy's apartment building. "I don't think I can eat for a week!"

"Mama Leila's food is always so good and plentiful. I won't have to make dinner for several days!" Maddy patted the care package that was sitting on her lap. "Thanks for the ride, Ash," she said as they pulled up to her apartment building. It was pretty quiet on Jasper Avenue on Sunday afternoons. Ashley easily found a spot to park right in front of the entrance.

"Anytime, Mads. You have a good week, okay?" Ashley instructed her as Maddy was stepping out of the car.

"Oh! I almost forgot!" Maddy said, jumping back onto the passenger seat.

"What? Did you leave a package in the backseat or something?" She looked on the seat behind Maddy but didn't see anything there. She waited for Maddy to elaborate, her eyebrows raised questioningly. Maddy seemed to be hesitating. She hemmed and hawed. Ashley tapped her long fingers on the steering wheel of her BMW. She watched as Maddy built up the courage to ask her whatever it was that she wanted to. 'This must be a big ask,' she thought.

"Chad invited me to his open house," Maddy finally said. "I feel like I have to make an appearance. I've been a bit... unfair to him in the past."

"It would be the grown-up thing to do," Ashley agreed. "That Netflix fiasco was not your best hour."

"I know. I'm embarrassed about that. I've changed since then. That's why I need to go."

'Here it comes,' Ashley thought.

'Here goes nothing,' Maddy thought.

"But I don't want to go alone," Maddy finally said with pleading eyes.

Neither of them spoke as Ashley stared at her, and Maddy smiled radiantly back. There was a silent stand-off in the car. Maddy was mentally willing Ashley. Ashley was trying hard to stand her ground. Ashley broke first.

"Fine, I'll be your plus one! Sheesh."

"Thank you, thank you!" Maddy said, giving her a goodbye hug. "You're the best, I owe you one!" she added, getting out of the car.

"Yes, you do, you really do," Ashley agreed. "You're starting to owe a lot of people, Ms. Maddy Whitman," she called out as Maddy shut the car door behind her and waved as she ran to her building's entrance.

AN HOUR LATER, MADDY had made herself a cappuccino and was sitting down at her dining room table. Staring at her open laptop, she tried to decide where to start to get caught up on work. Everything that had happened with Chef Mackenzie's murder and then the attempt on Tasha's life had naturally taken up almost all of her spare time. That was the time she usually concentrated on her administrative stuff. Things an assistant would do for her, if she could afford one. Since she could not and had to do all those chores herself, it meant that she had gotten quite behind. She still had a lot of items to go through, research, and list. Not to mention the trip she needed to take to the thrift store with items she wasn't interested in selling. She decided to start with her calendar and pulled it up. She typed in the things she needed to do this week and on which day she wanted to do them. On that list, she added 'Talk to PopPop about his dispensary.'

Out of the corner of her eye, she all of a sudden half saw, half felt a shadow go by her window. She looked up, there was nothing. She turned her attention back to her screen. A few minutes later, she heard a honking sound and looked out the window again just in time to see a Canada goose fly by. 'What the heck?' she thought. She stood up and walked over to the window at the same moment as the goose flew by again, this time heading in the opposite direction. 'Could it be?' she wondered. 'No! There's no way. It can't be Ryan! That's impossible.'

She grabbed her cell phone and snapped a couple of pictures of the goose as it flew by one more time. She then quickly called Zane and sent him a picture.

"Ryan has come to say goodbye!" she excitedly exclaimed as soon as he answered.

"What?"

"I'm at my dining room table, and Ryan is flying back and forth in front of my window. Look at the picture I just sent you."

"It can't be Ryan, Maddy. There are thousands and thousands of Canadian geese out there getting ready to fly south for the winter. And anyway, how would he know where you live?"

"Well, duh! He was born on my roof. He spent the first couple of weeks of his life on this building's rooftop, remember?" she said. "I'll send you a video."

She hung up. When the goose flew by again, she took a video of him. Maddy zoomed in on what was Ryan's deformed foot, the one that had stopped him from joining his family when they had flown away months ago.

She sent the video to Zane and then called him back.

"It's most definitely Ryan!" Her voice was trembling. "If you freeze the frame of him right in front of my window, you can see his foot and the bright orange tag the people at the sanctuary put on him!"

Maddy had sadly accepted that their previous drive out to the wildlife sanctuary had been their last visit with their sweet gander. Zane's friend, who worked at the sanctuary, told him a few days ago that the geese had started to fly around a lot and had left the sanctuary pond for the winter. Maddy was heartbroken, thinking she would never get the chance to see him again or even say goodbye.

"Well, would you look at that," Zane said after a few minutes. "I spotted his tag. It IS him!"

Maddy pressed her forehead gently against the window, staring out as Ryan circled back and flew in front of her again.

"Goodbye, sweet Ryan, be well." Her eyes were moist. "Oh, Zane, animals have a much simpler life than we do, don't they?"

"That they do, Maddy, that they do."

Chapter 26

SATURDAY

The week was over before she knew it. Maddy had accomplished most of what she had wanted to and felt pretty good about herself. She was now ready to go out and face Chad at his housewarming party. It was more than likely going to be a boring evening filled with his office colleagues. Wine and conversation with Ashley should make the evening bearable.

"You look very nice," Maddy said when she picked Ashley up at her apartment in Bugsy. Ashley wore a stunning shimmery top and black leather pants. Maddy could not wear skintight pants. A lot of people could not get away with wearing them. They seemed to amplify the wrong curves on her body. On Ashley's though, they looked like they had been painted on her.

"You don't look too shabby yourself," Ashley said, appraising Maddy's cute purple skirt and lilac top. "Is it new? It certainly makes you look fab-u-lous!"

"Yes, I had to splurge." Maddy perked up. Ashley's compliment made her feel much better about herself. She had spent hours shopping for the right outfit. "One can't show up at one's ex-boyfriend's house looking less than fantastic, don't you agree?"

"Absolutely! In fact, I think it is written in THE book of all books as one of THE top rules," Ashley responded.

"You mean the 'Hot Modern Woman's Rules to Living' one?"

"Do you know of any other book that matters?" Ashley asked with a chuckle.

"Nope. Good point," Maddy said cheerily.

They drove down the freeway singing along to their favorite music compilation. Something had been on Maddy's mind earlier, she now felt the urge to share it with Ashley.

"I can't believe Chad's finally getting his house and the white picket fence in suburbia. He never stopped talking about this very thing ever since I've known him."

Ashley looked over at her intently.

"Are you having any regrets about leaving him?"

"Oh, hell no," Maddy answered rather quickly. "We weren't compatible at all, and I wouldn't do well out in the 'burbs anyway. Sherwood Park is nice enough and everything, but I prefer downtown living."

"Yeah, I have a hard time picturing it myself," Ashley agreed. "But you sounded a bit melancholic when you said that. Perhaps you're a tad wistful then?"

"I don't think it's that. It's just... I don't know... Chad's making his dreams happen, you're doing what you always wanted to do - making a living working with art, Rick is totally rocking it at being a business owner, husband, and father." She hesitated a second before continuing. "I just sorta feel like everyone else is moving forward and I'm spinning my wheels, stuck in a rut and going nowhere."

"What are you talking about?" Ashley turned around so her whole body was facing Maddy. "You're pursuing your dream of owning a retail store. When those knives sell, you will be so close to owning it!"

"Yeah, when the knives sell. I have to wait until they're released by the police department. Remember what Zane said? Then we have to put them up for auction again."

"That just gives you a bit more time to come up with a name for your store," Ashley said. "It probably won't take more than six months or so."

"Speaking of names, I was thinking maybe 'Maddy's Madness.'"

"No."

"Okay, smartie pants, you're so quick to say no to my ideas. Why don't you try to come up with something then?"

"Sure, what about 'Lost Treasures'?"

"Oh. That is good," Maddy said begrudgingly.

They were just entering the hamlet of Sherwood Park when the traffic lights turned red. Maddy asked Ashley to enter the address on a map app on her cell phone so she could give her directions to Chad's new place.

"These darn street names make no sense! The 'trees' section, the 'bird' section, 'Foxboro' this and 'Foxboro' that." Ashley looked at her phone. "There's no rhyme nor reason to these names."

"I'm sure people who live here have it figured out." Maddy laughed.

"Yeah, well, I prefer street numbers. What if your phone wasn't working, or Google Maps was down?"

"We'd stop at a gas station or corner store and ask, like they did in the olden days. Come on. It's not that bad. Hey, we're already at another red light, and you still haven't given me the address of Chad's dream home."

"It's coming, it's coming," Ashley said. "I'll punch it into your phone."

"Okay, but you be the co-pilot and tell me where to go." It took Maddy a split second to hear what she had just said. She looked over at Ashley. "Don't say it, Ash. I know what you're thinking, 'I always have permission to tell you where to go, Maddy.' Yeah, yeah, yeah. You're such a smart Alec."

"That's 'Smart Ash' to you!" Ashley threw back with a laugh.

They were sitting at another red light on the east side of Baseline Road when Ashley noticed they needed to switch lanes.

"Oh crap, can you get over in the turn lane? You have to go left here!"

"Ashley!" Maddy, exasperated, shoulder-checked and managed to move over to the far-right lane. "I always forget how awful you are at giving directions."

"Hey, don't get mad at me! You didn't have to put me in charge of it, did you? Now turn left up here."

After a few more turns, they finally arrived in front of a taupe house with dark brown trim. There was a large, two-car garage that took up most of the sight line at the front of the house. Four cars were already in the driveway. A black wrought iron rod with a plaque hanging from it had the house's number on it. It was planted into the front lawn, which was very green and immaculately kept. Maddy wondered if it was real grass. Artificial grass would certainly be something Chad would put in, she thought.

They had to drive down several streets before they were able to find a parking spot. They got out and had to dodge a woman in a ponytail and baseball cap, jogging down the sidewalk, her Omega logo glinting in the sun.

Ashley went around to open the trunk and take out a bottle of wine they had brought as a housewarming gift.

"We could be drinking this in front of the Oilers game tonight," Ashley grumbled.

"Please don't remind me about missing the game. Showing up at Chad's open house is something I needed to do. Thanks again for coming with me, Ash." Maddy said, closing Bugsy's trunk for Ashley.

They strolled up to the house, noting the one obligatory tree in the middle of the front lawn that all new subdivisions seemed to require. Maddy looked down the street and saw house after house that looked almost identical to the one they were about to enter. Nope, no regrets here, she thought.

They strolled up the front walk and climbed the three steps to the small patio that had what looked like a brand-new wrought iron bistro set that matched the rod with the house number on it.

"Nice digs," Ashley said. The fact she stated, Maddy felt, needed to be followed by a 'but' after it. Ashley was much too polite to say anything else. They rang the doorbell, and in the deep recesses of the house, they heard the sound of the Westminster chimes. They looked at each other and burst out laughing. Of course, Chad would have chosen something pretentious, they both thought.

A moment later, the door swung open, and Chad stood there, wearing khaki pants, a turquoise golf shirt, a gold watch, and spotless dark blue loafers.

"Maddy! Ashley! I'm so glad you could come," he said, smiling and sounding truly genuine. "Come in, come in!"

They could hear jazz music playing in the background as he ushered them into the house.

"We brought you a bottle of wine," Maddy said, handing him the bottle. "A merlot, I remembered you like that grape."

"That's so thoughtful of you!" He took the bottle from her and turned around. His eyes scanned the room as though he were looking for someone. "My girlfriend loves this wine too, I'll introduce you as soon as I see her."

"That would be lovely," Maddy spoke up. She hoped her face didn't show her surprise that he was seeing someone. It wasn't that she cared. At all.

"She must be busy with some important clients of mine. She loves to mingle and get to know everyone. She has her own business, so she is probably networking as well, my little industrious sweetheart."

"I'm sure we'll meet," Ashley assured him.

He motioned for them to follow him across the room, approaching a wooden credenza full of bottles.

"Let me get you two some wine. Ashley, I believe you drink Malbec, don't you?"

"Yes, I'm surprised you remembered." Ashley took the full glass from his hand and brought it up to her lips. Maddy couldn't help but notice she had taken a pretty large swig.

"And here you go, Maddy, I know you don't care what kind of wine as long as it has some alcohol and comes in a bottle or even a box, am I right?" he broke into a robust round of laughter.

Maddy took the glass he offered her, barely keeping her composure, and smiled at him with tight lips. She began to wonder how she could accidentally spill some of that Malbec all over his pretentious shirt when Chad began to wave at someone behind them.

"Darling! Dumpling!" He was standing on his toes, looking over their shoulders and waving frantically, as though they were in a large arena and he might not be seen. "I want to introduce you to my friends, Love Bun!"

He squeezed between Maddy and Ashley as they began to turn around.

"Maddy, Ashley, here she is, my beautiful girlfriend. I think you three may even know each other..."

Maddy didn't have to come up with an idea on how to spill her wine as it spurted out all on its own.

Paris.

Pigeon Holed
Maddy Whitman Mystery Series Book 4

THE PARCHING DESERT heat clawed at her throat. Sand had replaced all moisture in her mouth. Out of habit, she attempted to wipe the ever-present sweat off her forehead with an already damp and dusty handkerchief. Her water canteen was empty, yet she still brought it up to her mouth, hoping there were a few drops of water left to cool her parched lips.

The crew gathered around the opening in the rock, their eyes darting back and forth, unspoken anticipation in their glances. Some rocked on the balls of their feet, trying to contain their excitement.

She wondered how many before her had walked by this location, not knowing what lay within. It hadn't been an easy find. A local Bedouin teenager, looking for baksheesh, had led her to the area. She hoped the monetary tip was worth the effort. It hadn't been easy, but her experienced team worked tirelessly for weeks, clearing out debris, searching for a way in.

She gestured to her foreman to lead her down the airless tunnel. Twenty feet below was a slab covered in hieroglyphics. She placed a gloved hand on its surface and mumbled something that sounded like a prayer. Stepping aside, she nodded. The foreman slowly slid the heavy slab far enough for them to squeeze into the airless chamber. She lifted her lantern around the room. The light bounced off the walls, and her breath caught in her throat. There wasn't one sarcophagus, but three.

"Da howah," she said, pointing toward the smallest sarcophagus. "That's the one."

Ahmad, the foreman, called two of his workers down. She watched them wrap the small sarcophagus in several cotton sheets, then in packing blankets. Ahmad went out first and dispersed the curious onlookers. Secrecy was of the utmost importance. A large wooden crate was brought to the opening. The workers carefully brought the sarcophagus out and placed it in the crate, then nailed it shut. Nobody would ever know of the small mummy's existence. It would be as if the desert had never surrendered it.

Coming in late 2025 'Pigeon Holed'

Sign up to receive release notifications https://bit.ly/3InJp4S

REVIEWS If you enjoyed this novel, please leave a review on Amazon or Goodreads, or wherever you buy your books.

Watch for more at www.facebook.com/[1]

Maddy Whitman Mystery Series
Fowl Play
Book 1

It's all fun and games until your goose gets cooked

Maddy Whitman, the sharp-witted aficionado of the storage auction world, is on a rollercoaster ride through hilarious mishaps and heart-pounding twists in "Fowl Play". When she stumbles upon a peculiar Mexican mask in a storage unit she bought at an auction, she unwittingly sets off a chain of events that lead her straight into the heart of a gripping mystery.

With danger lurking around every corner and a kidnapped woman's life on the line, Maddy must decode cryptic clues left by a cunning killer.

As tensions soar and the clock ticks, can she untangle the web of deception before it's too late? Packed with humour, suspense, and the irresistible charm of its female sleuth, "Fowl Play" is a must-read adventure that will leave you guessing until the very end.

Maddy Whitman Mystery Series
Lucky Ducky
Book 2

Art isn't priceless when you're a sitting duck!

The storage auction world is not always an exciting one. Yet life is anything but boring for Maddy as trouble and mayhem have a way of finding her. Follow her as she stumbles into a high-jinxed mystery involving kidnapped ducks, a multimillionaire's quirky ex-wife, and a long-lost grandfather who refuses to act his age.

As Maddy and her friends navigate the chaos in Edmonton, they encounter a cast of eccentric characters. Amidst all the turmoil, Maddy finds time to gain a fresh perspective on dating. But when she becomes the target of criminals, the stakes skyrocket. With time running out, can Maddy crack the case before it's too late? And will she ever date again?

An adventure-filled whodunit that will make you laugh and keep you in suspense until the very end.

Also by Monique MacDonald

Maddy Whitman Mystery
Fowl Play
Lucky Ducky
Quail's Tale

Also by Carla Howatt

Maddy Whitman Mystery
Fowl Play
Lucky Ducky
Quail's Tale

Standalone
For Crime's Sake: When True Crime Kills
For Love's Sake

Watch for more at https://www.facebook.com/CarlaHowattAuthor.

www.ingramcontent.com/pod-product-compliance
Lightning Source LLC
Chambersburg PA
CBHW030518020726
47494CB00004B/1138